The
Boathouse

The
Boathouse

Dane Anthony Howard

The Book Guild Ltd

First published in Great Britain in 2016 by
The Book Guild Ltd
9 Priory Business Park
Wistow Road, Kibworth
Leicestershire, LE8 0RX
Freephone: 0800 999 2982
www.bookguild.co.uk
Email: info@bookguild.co.uk
Twitter: @bookguild

Typeset in Aldine401 BT

Printed and bound in Great Britain by CPI Group (UK) Ltd, Croydon, CR0 4YY

ISBN 978 1910878 972

British Library Cataloguing in Publication Data.
A catalogue record for this book is available from the British Library.

To Francesca

The Young Entrepreneurs

A new business had opened on Parkway. It promised monkeys, talking parrots and reptiles for sale within. But the truth of the matter was that there weren't. None at all. For sale or otherwise. It was a deliberate deception. Anyone entering the premises expecting to peruse, select, and ultimately purchase any of the above could justifiably feel misled, aggrieved even. Not that anybody had entered with the intention of purchasing such exotic creatures. Certainly not since the new business opened. What was true however, the explanation, was that the new business, in fact an organic teahouse, was on a premises occupied for the previous fifty years by Palmer's Pet Shop, the new owners electing to retain the distinctive black and white embossed signage over the entrance: a little bit of heritage dating back to the early sixties, maybe even the late fifties. Returned to its former glory it remained eye-catching, quirky, and fully in keeping with the locale.

Instead of replacing it, the name of the new teahouse was an addition in bulbous letters sand-blasted into the former pet shop's floor-to-ceiling plate glass windows.

★ ★ ★

Long-standing residents of the area, at least those who bothered to follow such things, noted over the years that the pet shop had tried to move with the times, to adapt to changing tastes. It had stocked more conventional pets: rabbits, hamsters, tortoises. The latter however, given the fast pace of modern life and concomitant shorter attention spans, were never really likely to have a broad appeal amongst today's urban consumers. No one wanted the psychedelic tropical fish either: nice to look at, for a while, perhaps, but it wasn't long before all you noted were the gormless expressions, the soundless mouthings and general air of detachment. Fish, it seemed, were a bit thick. There was a further downside in that incompatible environmental media requirements proved to be an obstacle to any meaningful interaction between pet and owner: no cuddling, no stroking, no happy tail wagging. No silly animal voices. No ball games. Then there were the tiresomely particular aquatic requirements, not least the need to clean out and scrub the tank on a regular basis (where do you put the fish? Dry dock?). Point of fact, when you added it all up, the novelty of tropical fish was short-lived. Or perhaps they had just gone out of fashion. Either way, no one wanted them.

On occasion, not so very long ago, you could pass by the pet shop and see a litter of puppies, or kittens, semi-blindly crawling all over each other in a large cardboard box. The box placed in the shop window at ground level, carefully positioned to attract passers by who would stop to 'Ooh and Aah!' Targeted specifically at green-blazered children, the mid-afternoon primary kids on their way home from the school at the top of Parkway. Little fists clutching plastic folders with stickers bearing smudged names and form numbers in Roman numerals they didn't fully comprehend. Folders containing homework, and art destined for brief pride of place on a fridge door before being displaced by later period masterpieces. Yummy mummies on their way home to Primrose Hill, unable or unwilling to resist their child's pleading and tugging. Forced to detour, to push back wine o'clock so that little Seb or Chloe could press their noses to the pet shop window and exclaim excitedly, pointing at the furry cuteness of the tiny animals on the other side of the glass.

In what would turn out to be its final days, the pet shop did have a minor success. A swansong, but not involving swans. It had taken delivery of a litter of rare French bulldog puppies. Their bug-eyed, squashed faces and outsized ears had proved quite a draw. However, the little brass bell above the shop door seldom sounded as fewer and fewer people ventured inside, let alone bought anything. The French bulldogs, it turned out, had been the last hurrah: the pet shop's time had been and gone.

3

The young entrepreneurs behind the teahouse venture knew instinctively that they were onto something. They had their *'Eureka!'* moment when they recognised the increasing dissatisfaction they felt when served variable coffee invariably prepared by a heavily accented trainee 'barista'. Coffee in uninspiring, drearily homogeneous coffee shops, served in a corrugated cardboard cup topped with a plastic lid warning that the contents may be hot.

There had been an explosion of coffee shops over the past few years. The market was saturated and the young entrepreneurs reasoned there must be others out there, just like them, who would welcome a new hot beverage experience, even if they didn't yet know it. The answer, they decided, was to go back to the future, to re-invent a peculiarly British notion: the idea of sitting down to have a nice cup of tea. Who doesn't like that? But not an *'Olde English Tea Shoppe'*. What they envisaged was a modern take on the concept. They would accommodate the diverse, educated tastes of a new type of consumer. They would emphasise service, design and quality. They would promote healthy properties. They would be *organic!*

The young entrepreneurs undertook some perfunctory market research, visiting supermarkets, health stores, and other specialist shops in the area. Their instincts were soon confirmed. They were astounded by just how many different types of tea were out there.

There *is* a market; people actually do drink this stuff! They began to get excited about the idea, visualising it, extrapolating, riffing. They knew, for example, that a lot of business meetings, even job interviews in these days of zero-hours contracts, were held in the coffee shops they now began to actively despise. What they would be providing would be something different, something a bit more upmarket, not the tired old, 'Let's meet in the nearest *Nerocostalotobucks*' but, equally, not requiring the time-consuming ritual or expense of a business lunch. They could already picture it: the offer to meet in their teahouse would demonstrate imagination and flair on the part of the inviter, and make a favourable first impression on the invitee. Furthermore, the unique setting would be designed to afford them ready-made small talk, the perfect ice-breaker.

At the end of one of the early strategy meetings where ideas were thrashed out, one of the young entrepreneurs regaled the others with a scene from an old film where the actor Bob Hoskins' underworld character, recently released from a long spell in prison, is now minding a high-class prostitute off to the Ritz to meet a punter. Hoskins is clearly uncomfortable in the hotel surroundings, but he's determined to make sure his charge, whom he is a little bit in love with, is safe. Waiting in the lobby, Hoskins is approached by a haughty waiter in a swallow-tailed coat who enquires whether he may be of assistance. Hoskins thinks a moment before replying in broad cockney, 'Yeah. Cuppa tea mate?' The waiter, recognising this type of customer, raises an eyebrow and begins to reel off a long list of teas before Hoskins cuts him off, looks the idiot penguin up and down and says, 'Naaah. TEA!' The other young entrepreneurs had laughed, but quickly reassured themselves that things had changed, and they would be changing them further.

After scouting a few locations for their new organic teahouse, the young entrepreneurs decided Palmer's Pet Shop on Parkway would be the perfect place. It was conceived to be shabby-chic. Designed to attract the trendy, eclectic, yet fickle mix of inhabitants and workers in this part of north London. The 1970s-era sticky green vinyl floor was peeled away to reveal scarred wooden floorboards that were sanded, sealed and varnished. The lighting was industrial, from a factory in former Czechoslovakia. All-new wiring was surface-mounted, threaded through one and half inch aluminium tubes connected by right-angle elbow joints terminating in bakelite toggle switches. The walls were redecorated, an alternating mix of distressed concrete, distemper, and flock wallpaper. The furniture was sourced from local antique shops, flea markets, the Internet. Chairs were deliberately mismatched: bentwoods, ladder backs, wing backs, stacking, club. They bought once modish, now post-ironic black leather sofas, button-backed Chesterfields, there was even a chaise longue, for those possessing the requisite self confidence. A job lot of unforgiving wooden chairs were rescued from a nearby Methodist chapel, ones with a pocket at the back for hymn books and those bibles with the tissue-paper thin pages and tiny, double columned print. And, more recently, stuffed with cheaply produced flyers on primary-coloured paper. Flyers advertising charity events that only a handful of people ever attended, the same handful of people. The most recent addition to the teahouse had been one of those old-fashioned gym benches which, despite its nostalgic charm, was only ever sat upon when there was absolutely nowhere else available, and even then only as a temporary perch, the customer retaining a tight grip on their tray, constantly scanning the room, primed for rapid reaction should other, more comfortably-seated customers betray any sign that they were about to depart.

It followed that the tables were just as mismatched as the chairs.

* * *

In the space of less than twelve months the idea had germinated, then gestated, and now it was born. The shop was fully fitted out and the staff: managing, specialist, waiting, had all been recruited. The new organic teahouse on Parkway was a reality, proudly offering over thirty different types of tea. There were the black teas: English Breakfast; Assam; Darjeeling; Earl Grey; Midnight Grey; Lapsang Suchong; Pu Erh; Russian Caravan; Notting Hill; Blueberry Hill; Absolute Cinnamon; Soho Spice; Caramel Sweetheart; Walk In the Wood; and Chai Black. There were green teas: Precious Dew; Pinhead Gunpowder; Dragon

Well. Red ones, or rooibos, from South Africa (though like chamomile, technically speaking not teas at all, produced, as they are, from *Aspalathis lineraris*, not *Camellia sinensis*). Finally there were rare white teas from China. Teas made from young buds specially harvested in the springtime: White Snow; White Monkey; White Dragon.

The new teahouse offered coffee too, along with a wide variety of sandwiches and cakes. Scones were served with generous dollops of strawberry jam and cream. Everything was freshly made on the premises and laid out temptingly on a long wide counter that ran almost half the length of the room. In the earliest days, an aproned employee would be stationed outside on the pavement, a large plate balanced in one hand. There to offer samples to the general public, an attempt to get them to come in for more, or at least become aware of the existence of the new teahouse. But the general public proved reluctant to accept free food from someone standing in the middle of the pavement, a stranger seeking attention, trying to make eye contact, forcing them to change course, avoid a physical coming together: there was probably a catch they thought, perhaps a guiltily-extracted direct debit to a food bank? Besides, the general public were busy, they were in a hurry, preoccupied, deep in thought, unable to consider an unscheduled break from whatever it was they were hurrying towards. This was London, after all.

* * *

It was London, that was true, but this particular part of London was one of those places where everyone, from whatever walk of life or background, just got on with each other. Tolerance and acceptance were the defaults. The culmination of an enriching diversity and one of the multifarious attractions of Camden Town. The London village where the Northern Line, running directly under it, became pinched at the waist. Two branches fused to present a choice: 'City', or 'West End'? A melting pot of English, Irish, Greeks, Somalis, Poles, and increasingly French, Russians, even Japanese. The very rich and the very poor living within a stone's throw of each other. Grand stuccoed villas in the shadows of sometimes squalid council estates. Famous people living cheek by jowl with a majority destined forever to remain unremarked. An area that had grown to fill the space between the rail termini of Euston and St Pancras/Kings Cross to the south, and the genteel, greener heights of Belsize Park and Hampstead in the north. A place where you could be whatever you wanted to be. Do whatever you wanted to do. Re-invent yourself. Assume a new identity. Inhabit a niche role. Somewhere you could dress to impress at weekends. A place where, however outrageous your appearance, actions, or intentions, it was more than likely that no one would bat an eyelid, or miss a beat. It was a place where you could just be.

Colourful characters abounded in Camden Town. Most harmless, like the fat guy ('Are you *sure* he's a guy?'), the one with the long yellow straw wig tied on with a kerchief, the one who wore aviator sunglasses, whatever the weather. Always with the same, empty 'bag for life' (the possible symbolism of this subject of debate in the local pubs, no one quite able to come down on one side or the other). But the nice thing to see was that he was accorded respect: no one made fun of him. He was what he was. No gang of disenfranchised youth had ever taken their frustration out on him.

The characters weren't all entertaining though. A total nutter had appeared recently. A guy in dirty ripped clothing, staggering around in the high street, talking to himself whilst simultaneously beating his head and chest with implausible savagery. Self harm and loathing. You felt sorry for him in a 'There but for grace of God go I' sort of way, but you had stuff to do. You gave him a wide berth, he clearly had issues, but you were busy.

The general maxim though was live and let live: so long as you weren't rude, or overtly threatening, you wouldn't be judged or discriminated against. You would be taken as you were found.

The aproned-guy on the pavement with the tray proved unnecessary: the teahouse had been embraced immediately, virtually an overnight success. It was not long before the mismatched chairs and tables were fully occupied by a sundry crowd of arty, media and business types who would find themselves rubbing shoulders (if nothing else) with MILFs rocking SUV-sized buggies, carelessly blocking the thoroughfares, and tourists drawn by the zoo, or the world famous market. And then there were those who might be described as

'Other'. Or, perhaps more accurately, members of a peculiar collective. Individuals probably best filed under the golf-sized umbrella of 'Camdenites'. But irrespective of tribe, the teahouse's new and ever-growing customer base all had one thing in common: everyone had a laptop, a tablet, or a smart phone, usually at least two, sometimes all three devices. If they weren't talking to their companions (or even if they *were* talking to their companions), they would be bent forwards, hunched over, constantly checking and pecking a screen or a keyboard: email, Facebook, WhatsApp, Twitter, Snapchat, Instagram, Tinder, Grindr, 3nder - swiping left and right. YouTube mash-ups, hashtag this, hashtag that. Liking, disliking. What's been tweeted, re-tweeted, what's trending? What's gone viral?

But the aphorism is true, appearances can be deceptive. Who would have guessed that the rather plump, aggressively made-up Goth girl with the eyebrow and lip piercings, sitting there on her own in the corner, head to toe in black, was a shy convent-educated young lady up for the day from Hertfordshire who had ordered a jasmine green tea specifically for its antioxidants, extra chlorophyll content and thermo genesis calorie burning benefits, to go with her raspberry muffin.

★ ★ ★

It was here, the new organic teahouse on Parkway that Ben and Louise were destined shortly to meet.

- II -

Ben

Ben left Regent's Park. He'd walked all the way from Oxford Street, up through Marylebone where the predominant language on the street these days appeared to be French. Ben enjoyed this: there's only one thing sexier than a French woman speaking French he thought, and that's a French woman speaking English. He recalled a delightful exchange where a pretty young French shop assistant had informed him that everything was 'Alf price' and enquired if he would like his 'receept' in the bag.

It was dusk. They'll be doing the rounds soon Ben thought, padlocking the gates with those heavy chains. Why do they do this in Regent's Park when they don't do it on Primrose Hill? Primrose Hill, originally a meadowland, part of the land Henry VIII confiscated from the monastries during the Reformation and had decreed should be a public space, but where the eponymous pale yellow flowers, *primula vulgaris*, no longer bloomed, and attempts to reintroduce them over the years proved to be as successful as those to put a nightingale in Berkeley Square.

Primrose Hill, the site of many duels in the early 1800s. Pistols at dawn. Seconds and surgeons in close attendance. Where Welsh druids gathered during the solstice, and Blake had a vision of the sun, 'I have conversed with the spiritual Sun,' he said, 'I saw him on Primrose Hill'.

Ben considered that Blake may have succumbed to sunstroke during this little chat, he was manifestly befuddled, or on something, for he went on to write,

The fields from Islington to Marylebone,
To Primrose Hill and Saint John's Wood,
Were builded over with pillars of gold,
And there Jerusalem's pillars stood.

Okay, there's a large Jewish population in this part of London, but Jerusalem? And the repetition of 'pillars'. Oh dear.

On the hill where Paul McCartney, out walking with dear Martha, met the fool. And the Rolling Stones, having been up all night recording, and looking like it, went to be photographed for the cover of an LP. Where, in 'The War of the Worlds', Martian invaders consolidated their gains and began ingesting the locals, and from whose summit Pongo barked a warning over London about Cruella de Vil's evil schemes.

★ ★ ★

For an unsurpassed view in other cities thought Ben, you scale a building, but in London you climb a hill. A hill where, on summer evenings, laughter cascades from small groups enjoying picnics and sharing bottles of wine; the cloying smell of marijuana is suspended in the air, and the Victorian lamps studding the paths remain lit all night, everything very much *laissez-faire*.

I should be a poet thought Ben, as John and Beverley Martyn's song 'Primrose Hill' popped into his head. He loved that sax solo.

* * *

With the whirring of the tractor-drawn lawnmower, the first cut of the year, still resounding in his ears, Ben crossed at the traffic lights by the celebrity chef gastro pub. It was still early spring but, to Ben's mind, nothing evoked a British summer more than the smell of just-cut grass. He found himself wondering what lay ahead as the days grew longer, warmer. At the same time he was transported back to a bucolic childhood in Cambridgeshire. The big house on the river that his dad was doing-up, still, after all these years. Those long light evenings when he would be sent upstairs and lie there in his narrow bed, unable to sleep. The window open, the drawn but ineffective curtains gently billowing in the summer breeze, like unrestrained canvas on a small sailboat. Ben could still visualise his father mowing the lawn with the ancient, but lovingly tinkered with orange and green Suffolk Colt lawnmower. The regimented two-tone stripes. What would it have been, nine, ten o'clock in the evening? The sound of the lawnmower growling louder as it advanced, dropping to a mutter as it turned and retreated. An unlikely lullaby, waves on a seashore, soothing Ben into sleep.

Dusk was Ben's favourite time of day. He found it romantic: colours and shapes increasingly indistinct. A dusty tiredness descending over the streets. Sounds and smells coming to the fore, competing with sight for top spot in the hit parade of the senses. A twilight world where the events and exertions of the day were gradually cloaked, substituted by a promise of nocturnal adventure! Definitely maybe.

★ ★ ★

Ben was heading home down Parkway, Camden Town. Note: Camden *Town*. Like other residents, Ben would metaphorically shake his head whenever it was abbreviated to 'Camden'. Camden was the name of a large north London borough, not the gloriously vibrant place where he lived.

Ben loved Parkway which, less than one hundred and fifty years ago, was just a track through fields known as Slip Shoe Lane. He found it fascinating. It was forever reinventing itself. Nothing stayed the same for long. Shops and businesses came and went with increasing frequency. There was always something new to explore or experience. At the park end, steel and glass apartments were being constructed. The garish 'Quik

15

Fit Exhaust Centre' had gone and a new building had shot up, aggressive scalene triangle shaped balconies jutting out from every floor, like the spines of a startled hedgehog. A man in a hard-hat and 'hi-viz' jacket was descending on a yellow scissor lift, working late thought Ben. An irregular high-pitched burst of power tools reached him from somewhere deep within the new building, scything through the din of the traffic. Cars and buses were being brought to a halt to allow a concrete mixer, a lumbering monster bumblebee, to emerge tentatively, almost shyly from the site as though ashamed of its corpulence, taking its place apologetically in the line of traffic rumbling slowly down the street. Beyond was the seemingly endless parade of estate agents with their fantastical house prices. Ben rented, and wondered if he would ever be able to afford to buy in this neighbourhood?

He walked on, past the Dublin Castle, self-styled 'legendary music venue', a proving/killing ground for many Britpop bands. The smell of stale beer hit him as he passed the entrance. Ben peeked inside but couldn't see who was bashing away with reckless abandon on a drum kit, the percussive sound punctuated by the crash of a Hi-hat. Next door was the second-hand record store, the window adorned with iconic LP covers featuring bananas, zips, a mustachio'd fab four in psychedelic satin uniforms, a white face painted with a streak of lightning, and one with day-glo ransom note graphics exhorting people to pay no heed to the 'Bollocks'.

Outside 'Unwins' the wine merchant (est. 1843,

boarded up 2012), the road narrowed as the pavement widened to accommodate a newly installed row of ungainly Boris bikes. Just beyond was Ben's favourite shop, a greengrocers run by a rotund, jolly Turk called Cem. Inside was a riotous display of exotic fruits, the sweet aromas of Italian lemons, Dutch apples, French apricots, pomegranates from Chile, mangoes from the Dominican Republic, satsumas from South Africa. Towards the back, the smells became earthier, commonplace: fourteen different types of potato, thirteen of tomato, eight of mushrooms, seven types of carrot and two of artichokes. There were odd-shaped vegetables Ben didn't recognise. When the shop first opened, Ben suggested Cem should really consider calling it 'Aladdin's Fruit and Veg Cave', this place where on more than one occasion Ben had struggled with an urge to stroke the soft fuzz on the peaches, restrained by a fear that he might be observed, his behaviour misconstrued. Cem asking him to leave.

Then there were all the restaurants: tapas, pizza, bistro, bento. Tables and chairs spilling out onto the pavement. Pubs too. Smokers standing around outside in huddled groups, puffing faster as the mercury shrank. Publicly shamed yet defiant. Drawing comfort from within an informal support group. The knowledge that, at least for now, they were not alone.

Ben checked out the week's films at the multi-screen Odeon, and forthcoming performances at the 'Jazz Café'. Beyond the nail 'parlour' and the 'Paradise' dry-cleaners was the travel agent. Ben couldn't fathom how it managed to survive, not with all the wwwdotinternetdotthingdotcom-petition these days. Then there was the fresh flower stall (is there any *other* kind? Slightly wilted? Stale? Dead?), where you could inhale heady fragrances as you passed and hear the crisp clipping of secateurs as the stallholder trimmed and deftly wrapped blooms and foliage into paper cones in one fluid movement. Beyond Parkway, at the junction with the High Street and Chalk Farm Road, Ben could see the tube station, its overcrowded exit a production line spitting out a constant stream of humanity through the automatic gates. But Ben didn't go that far: he made an abrupt left turn, climbed two steps, and pushed at the door of the new organic teahouse.

★ ★ ★

Ben was becoming a regular, corroborating the prescience of the young entrepreneurs. He looked forward to popping in after work, to reflect upon the day before heading home to his one-bedroomed flat. The first time he noticed the teahouse, he couldn't help but wonder what had happened to Palmer's pets, the unsold stock. The animals and birds, the snakes, the insects? Had there been a closing down sale? He had missed it. Had there been special offers? 'Half price hamsters? Free ferret with every purchase?' Or had they all been secretly released back into the wild and were right now crawling and slithering around bewilderedly in the park? Or had they been put down? Death at dawn. A midnight massacre? If so, Ben wondered how *anyone* could do this. Then, literally, *how* anyone could do this. Ben often had thoughts like these.

★ ★ ★

There was something about the process that appealed to Ben. The selection and weighing of the loose-leaf tea, the clever design of the teapot, how it fitted neatly on top of the china white cup and saucer, the tea strainer. A real spoon. How the brewing process forced you to sit back and relax, take your time, savour the experience. Not quite the ritual performance of a Japanese tea ceremony perhaps thought Ben, though, if pressed, he had little idea what this entailed beyond picturing in his mind's eye an overly made-up, crimson-lipped and kimono'd geisha girl kneeling subserviently, a backdrop of sliding paper screens decorated with watery representations of snow-topped mountains, Hokusai's Wave, fire-breathing dragons, and small groups of little people in traditional dress, oval faces, eyes and mouths single curved lines, standing around apparently unconcerned by the dragons – or was he getting confused with the Chinese? Plinky-plonk music in the background accompanied by, to his ears, a high-pitched toneless wailing. At a dark-laquered table with amputated legs, eyes lowered demurely and thick black hair pinned into a bun by knitting needles, a geisha delicately folding back her silky sleeves and proposing to her male client, a buttoned-up salary man or, more likely, a wealthy industrialist, that she be 'mother'.

★ ★ ★

Unlike many of the teahouse's clientele, Ben did not have any piercings, nor did he have a beard, or any facial hair for that matter. He did have a tattoo however: a symbol on his right ankle. A pictogram he understood to be an ancient symbol representing the sun. It was only some months later, climbing the steps to the cabin of a low-cost jet parked out on the apron, that he noted it was identical to the swirly white squiggle revolving slowly on the turbo fan engine. Ben didn't mind though, it made him smile, he still liked it. Sun *and* travel.

Although an IT consultant for a mobile telephone advertising company, Ben was no geek. He was a popular guy, a fun guy. He had an endearing mischievous streak. 'Ben?' They would say, 'Yeah, good bloke.' That was the general consensus. One of his passions was music, all sorts, from classic to club, madrigals to Motown, jazz to rock, rap to reggae. He loved lyricists and proselytized about what he referred to as the 'Holy Trinity': Tom, Nick... and Bob (Waits, Cave, Dylan). Ben had grown up with music: his mother had been a pianist, she had studied at the Royal Academy and was once even auditioned by BBC radio when still in her early twenties. But then ill health had struck, leaving her unable to practice. Her nascent career brought to a cruel halt. But she would never forget, and neither would anyone else, not least her husband, that she could have found fame and fortune as a professional pianist.

At home, Ben grew up to a soundtrack of classical music. There was something about Johann Sebastian: the harpsichord, the violin, and the cello concerti that resonated. He was unable to articulate it, but there was something that attracted him, something almost mathematical about the composition. He also grew to admire Prokofiev and Mahler, but a particular favourite was Rimsky-Korsakov's 'Scheherazade', the grandiosity transporting him on a magic carpet to a fantasy land governed by cruel yet handsome potentates: swarthy men in turbans, reclining, voluminous trousers tied at the ankle like MC Hammer, their feet in curly slippers; harems of diaphanously-robed bathing beauties watched over by impassive Nubian eunuchs; slaves and scimitars; bejewelled belly dancers wearing numerous veils, demanding heads…

There had been a brief period when Ben deliberately antagonised his mother by repeatedly playing Mahler's 'Kindertotenlieder' as loud as he dare on their old record player, a petty act of defiance, a response to a scolding. Ben could not remember when, but his mother had once translated the title of the record as 'Songs for Dead Children'. He'd felt slightly disconcerted at the time, hadn't known why she felt the need to tell him this. He hadn't asked her, he just liked the sing-song title which reminded him of the chocolate eggs, the ones with the little toy inside.

Whenever he heard his mother coming to demand that he turn it down, as he knew she would, she would find Ben gazing into the middle distance, lost in melancholy thought, or totally absorbed in reading the back of the yellow and black Deutsche Grammophon record sleeve, even though it was all in German.

Despite his early exposure and appreciation of classical music, Ben did not play an instrument. There had been a short while, he must have been about eight or nine, when he was forced to learn the piano. Made to practice for an hour every day on his mother's old Bechstein upright, all alone in the chill of the barely-used dining room while his parents were cosily watching the TV next door. It had been a punishment for shoplifting.

It had been the summer holidays. Ben had been out with his mother, a voracious reader, returning some books to the library. Afterwards they had gone opposite to look around the toyshop, a bribe to ensure Ben would accompany her uncomplainingly. Ben's mother telling him that maybe Father Christmas might bring him something or other, if he was good. They were on their way out, he could see the door. Ben's heart had been in his mouth, they were almost clear. Then the shop owner, arms folded, appeared out of nowhere, barring the way. Ben was caught red-handed: stuffed into his pocket was an unpaid for 1:43 scale model car, a two-tone Chevrolet Impala with twin headlights, working doors, hood and trunk. It was American. The steering wheel was on the other side. It had caught

Ben's eye and he desperately wanted it. He needed it right now but knew his mother wouldn't buy it for him. Not today. He couldn't wait until Christmas. What else could he have done?

Ben's mother was absolutely mortified, for a moment believing the shopkeeper was accusing her of being complicit in the attempted theft. Ben, hot tears of shame spilling down his cheeks, handed over the toy car, fearfully placing it in the now outstretched palm of the shopkeeper. Outside, for the first and only time in his life, Ben's mother struck him. A succession of head-jolting blows that made him whimper and cower like a dog, right there in the street. Other pedestrians, shocked by this violence right in front of them, tut-tutted disapprovingly yet knew better than to step in and remonstrate with a semi-hysterical woman dragging a child along. Ben felt shock rather than physical pain. When they reached home, Ben did not need to be ordered twice by the silently quivering finger of his mother: using all-fours he scampered straight up to his room where it was clear that he was to wait until his father came home.

* * *

Ben heard him pull up in the driveway. The usually reassuring metallic opening and closing of the car door followed by that of the back door. He climbed off his bed and crept out onto the landing. At the top of the stairs, crouched down, both hands gripping the newel post, Ben strained unsuccessfully to decipher the outraged stage whispers reaching him from below, knowing his parents were discussing his crime and punishment. Ben heard his father's footsteps, pictured him in his polished brogues, striding across the kitchen and into the hall, the sudden ominous silence as tiles gave way to shag pile. Ben flew back to his bedroom.

Ben looked up slowly. His father filled the doorway. He just stood there, looking in at him. He doesn't appear to be too angry thought Ben as, in a careworn voice Ben was told that with immediate effect he was banned from entering shops for a whole year. He would have to wait outside, or sit in the car. He could no longer be trusted. He had let his mother and father down. He would end up in jail if he wasn't careful. He'd brought disgrace upon the family.

"Do you realise what you've done? Your mother will never be able to show her face in that shop again. Do you know what this means?"

Ben didn't, and his father failed to elaborate. Ben hung his head as though in shame. In reality though it was to mask the relief that had swept through him at the leniency of the sentence. Ben hoped his head hanging conveyed abject repentance, but his father, who knew Ben better than Ben knew himself, was not so easily fooled. He could tell that Ben was thinking he had been let off lightly: what boy wants to go shopping with his parents anyway? But what Ben's father didn't know, what he would have been shocked to learn, was that Ben immediately recognised that this ban would not prevent him from going into shops and nicking stuff when his parents weren't around. He would still be able to go in and get sweets and comics with his mates. But then came the second part. The bit about the piano.

* * *

Not unreasonably, Ben's mother considered the discipline required to play a musical instrument would be good for Ben. It had done her no harm, after all. It would improve him. It would help keep him out of trouble. However, whilst Ben acknowledged that it would be quite good if he could play something, and was even intrigued by aspects of notation: quavers, semi or otherwise, the breves, crotchets, the minims, it was just too difficult. Learning the piano was not fun. He would rather be doing something else. He simply couldn't practice for an hour every day. It was too, too boring.

Ben would find himself clock-watching as he practiced scales at ever-increasing intervals. He would look over his shoulder and will the hands around the face of the grandfather clock in the far corner, its slow-swinging pendulum seemingly drawing out the hour rather than ushering it to a close. There had been a brief moment when Ben toyed with the idea of physically forwarding the minute hand round a couple of inches, but he couldn't reach it without dragging the piano stool across the room, and there was a real risk of being caught during one of his mother's surprise inspections. Ben began to hate the annoying tick of the metronome too, never fully understanding its purpose. And Beethoven, his mother's hero, stern-faced and unblinking, an alabaster bust on top of the piano staring down at him. Good job he's deaf thought Ben.

A couple of weeks into his sentence, the family were sat around the table at supper when Ben made an announcement. Convinced in his own mind his parents would concur, Ben said that he considered he'd given it a fair go, but had reluctantly come to the conclusion that the piano was not his forte. Ben was rewarded by an involuntary chuckle from his father. His mother on the other hand, apart from a clattering of cutlery against china, made no response.

However, excuses were found and increasingly accepted and, after a couple more weeks, the insistence on weekly lessons and daily practice was gradually relaxed before quietly being dropped altogether. Ben's parents choosing to believe that Ben had, literally, been taught a lesson (or rather lessons), and Ben believing he had forced his parents into a sort of sonic submission. Ben retained a passion as a consumer, but he would never go near a musical instrument ever again.

- III -

More about Ben

Ben was surprised by how much money he was beginning to accrue through a clause in his contract that awarded him a percentage for every sale of the software his team had developed.

Over the past few weeks there had been a string of successes. It was turning out to be true, success bred success. A sales drive involving name-dropping a list of up-and-coming businesses had resulted in a handful of blue chip customers signing on the dotted line. The culmination of a successfully devised strategy to personally target influential individuals, to play on human fears and insecurities: an unspoken accusation of complacency in today's evolving market; not being sufficiently forward looking in the face of hungrier competitors; not keeping abreast of technological change; a fear of being sacked.

The campaign was paying handsomely. The blue chips likewise.

The company Ben worked for breathlessly advertised itself as a 'global mobile and tablet advertising solution provider employing audience profiling in a mobile environment to allow businesses to target individuals directly with related ads over a variety of different platforms through accessing individual telephone subscribers' internet activity.'

Ben had been taken on to head up the small team specifically for his interpersonal skills, rather than as another pointyhead. Someone to attend meetings and bridge the divide between potential client and the otherwise socially inept computerists they relied upon.

Ben's team had adapted and built on existing technology, web-browsing software already Orwellian in scope, to develop the new tool. He marvelled at the general public's ignorance or, worse, indifference towards the amount of information about them that was out there, never to be removed. Information covering virtually every aspect of an individual's life. Theoretically accessible to anyone determined enough to obtain it, be it with good or malign intentions. But did people really care? Did it really matter, if you're not breaking the law? What about all the indisputable advantages? The convenience, the connectivity. The immediacy. Not forgetting all the fun aspects of living life 'online'.

★ ★ ★

The commercial success of Ben's company was almost entirely down to the efforts of one person, Natalie, the owner and director. A smart Jewish businesswoman universally known as 'Gnat' due to her diminutive size, but also an ironic comment on an irrepressible force of nature. An undeniably charismatic client-facing owner. Pocket-sized yet larger than life. A sexy 37-year-old married woman. A woman to whom it was very difficult to say 'no'. To deny. A woman who, when Ben first joined was warned with a wink and a nudge by co-workers of both sexes, exercised a sort of female *droit du seigneur* over her employees.

Ben thought they were teasing him, the 'new boy'. But even if there were an element of truth in what they said, Ben, having landed this exciting career opportunity, determined that he would not jeopardise it with any ill-considered sexual and/or romantic involvement with the boss. Ben vowed to remain professional. However, like many before him, he caved. He fell at the first hurdle.

★ ★ ★

It happened a couple of weeks in. One of the regular after work parties in The Mockingbird, the pub near the office, just off Oxford Street. Ben was there with a group of colleagues from the industry. Gnat was there too, a social animal partial to New Zealand Sauvignon Blancs but a distinct lightweight when it came to alcohol consumption: just two or three glasses

29

producing a deleterious effect. Ever pragmatic though, Gnat had discovered that a line or two of cocaine was the perfect antidote.

During these get togethers, these long evenings, Gnat would disappear two or three times with a 'chosen one', aka 'the anointed', to snort a line or two delivered by the east London Vietnamese dealers she had on speed dial.

As this particular evening wore on, Gnat turned predatory. She had been table-hopping all evening without appearing to acknowledge Ben's existence before suddenly plonking herself down on his bench, playfully pushing into him and, with an arm around his shoulder, pulled him close and whispered into his ear a staccato of overly enunciated words.

"Ben. Come. With me. I need… speak to you."

"What? Tell me here."

"I can't. You need… Come with me."

"Really?"

Ben heard himself sounding whiny, pathetic, already defeated.

Gnat left just as suddenly as she had arrived. Tottering away on impossibly high heels along a well-worn route, not bothering to glance back, certain he would follow. To Ben, left sitting there, she had appeared completely sober. He decided he had no option but to obey his boss's command. As he made a move to stand, he staggered slightly, striking his knee against the table leg before catching the knowing look of one of his team who raised his drink in a silent toast, a broad grin on his face. Ben became conscious of others watching, but was unable to make out whether they were gloating or jealous. One of them, someone he knew only slightly but felt sure he didn't like, made a 'trot along' sign with his fingers. And Ben did, a helpless lamb to the slaughter.

She was waiting for him in a narrow corridor, right opposite the ladies. She grabbed his arm, pulled him forwards and down. She planted a quick kiss on his cheek.

"C'mon Ben, we're going in here."

"What? Why? Is this a good idea Gnat? There may be someone in there."

Ben knew that she knew that he knew. Gnat pushed open the door, pulling him proprietorialy in after her, past the hand basins, towards a cubicle at the end of a row. Ben caught a glimpse of himself in the harsh light reflected in the mirror. He looked ridiculous. What was he doing? Yet at the same time, strangely, it seemed quite normal. True, Gnat was married, but that was surely her concern. Ben was single. He had not yet met Louise. She was still in the future. Louise, who would be the love of his life. The woman who would change everything. Forever. It would be a further three weeks before he met Louise.

Luckily, or not, the ladies loo was empty. Gnat closed the door of the stall and turned the lock. On tip-toes she put her arms around Ben's neck and, a faraway expression on her face, closed her eyes and began kissing him. Surprisingly soft kisses. Then she began to push his lips apart with her tongue. A further surprise: her tongue was rough, just like a cat. A tongue designed to lap milk. Gnat the cat thought Ben.

Ben had been on his third pint and Gnat, if not conventionally pretty (her nose was a bit crooked), was certainly far from unattractive. He fancied her and found himself responding. What else could he do? Anyway it was harmless adult fun, a right of passage. It would all be forgotten about, dismissed with laughter in the morning. Wouldn't it?

Ben was not quite prepared for what happened next though. Gnat began taking her top off, her arms crossed, lifting it above her head, before it became snagged on an earring. It never entered Ben's head to try to stop her, to reason with her, instead he instructed her to be careful. He actually helped her remove the garment. Underneath she was wearing a nude bra. This was next to come off, unfastened and dropped to the floor where it joined her top. She started kissing Ben again, pressing herself against his chest. Ben pushed her back against the melamine wall of the cubicle which shook alarmingly but held. They carried on. Ben bent down and took a breast in his mouth, and was about to move on to the other one when Gnat pushed him away forcefully. She reached down to her handbag and produced a tiny sealed plastic bag covered with $ signs.

Turning away from Ben, and with practiced ease, Gnat quickly chopped out two lines on the top of the cistern with her Oyster card then, from nowhere, a cut off plastic straw appeared in her hand. Gnat steadied herself, and with feet planted firmly apart, bent forwards from the waist over the toilet bowl, lowering her face to within a centimetre of the ceramic cistern, the straw in her right nostril, the left one shut off with a forefinger.

Behind her, Ben was focussing unsteadily on the red outline of a bra imprinted on pale skin. He leant forward to put his arms around her in an embrace, intending to kiss her on the side of the neck, but he couldn't reach. She was bent too far forward. Ben lost his balance. Either through too much to beer, or simply carried away by the moment, Ben found himself toppling forward, his puckered lips about to land in the hollow between Gnat's shoulder blades just as she gave a big snort and straightened sharply, catching Ben completely unawares.

A prominent vertebra struck Ben painfully, right on the bridge of his nose. He blinked. His eyes smarted and he became momentarily disorientated. Gnat, oblivious to his plight, wiped the residual powder with a swipe of a finger and rubbed it into her gums with a rapid, violent gesture. Then, without even looking at him, handed the straw to Ben. It was his turn. Again, what could he do? Gathering his senses, Ben conducted a rapid assessment of the situation: his boss had just kissed him. With her tongue. She was now standing there, topless, making no attempt to cover herself (how often does she do this?), offering him a class A drug. Ben had never taken cocaine before but was concerned it might appear churlish to refuse. He took the straw and they shuffled awkwardly, exchanging places within the narrow confines of the cubicle.

Ben could smell it before he felt a peculiar arid sensation as he hoovered up the powder. It stung his septum. He could feel it dropping down into the back of his throat.

When Ben stood up again, Gnat had retrieved her clothes. She was putting them back on. What was going on? She wouldn't let him kiss her. She was holding him off now, using both arms, at one point even twisting his fingers backwards, surprisingly strong, making him wince. Gnat unlocked the door and stepped out, adjusting her clothes and hair in the mirror.

"I'm staying in town tonight. Let's go to this bar I know. Now go. Quickly!"

Ben was shooed out of the toilet, past a surprised-looking woman heading in the opposite direction who turned to watch him go, double-checking the sign on the door.

Back in the bar, the numbers were thinning out as the after work crowd began to head for their trains. Ben ordered another pint and waited for Gnat to join him. He felt himself being swept along, surrendering control, not necessarily unpleasantly. What next? He began to feel a rush in his head. He felt emboldened. His pint remained untouched.

Out on the street, Gnat put her arm through Ben's and hailed a black cab to take them to Victoria. He noted she was not wearing her wedding ring. When had she taken it off? Paying the driver she led Ben through the commuter crowds to a nearby hotel where she instructed Ben to go and sit on a chair in the lobby while she, Gnat, unburdened by luggage, brazenly booked a double room for the night. This done, she click-clacked across the marble lobby towards Ben, grinning, oblivious, or more likely unconcerned, by the concierge's stare.

Gnat pointed up a grand sweeping staircase which led to a dimly-lit wood-panelled bar on the mezzanine floor.

"Let's go and get another drink."

That night turned out to be the first of three matings, all initiated by Gnat. She had asserted her right and then things had fizzled out. Any fleeting thoughts Ben might have entertained about being the unfortunate victim of sexual harrassment in the workplace (had things really come to this?) were dispelled. In getting to know Gnat, er, better, he discovered that she was actually a genuinely warm and caring person. It hadn't been unpleasant sleeping with her, on the contrary, nevertheless he was glad it was over and, fortunately, their working relationship remained unaffected.

- IV -

Ben cont'd

Increasing affluence meant that Ben was able to buy his first car. He didn't need one of course, living in the centre of London, but along with music, cars, specifically older cars, classic cars, was another of his passions. He kept a stash of car porn in his flat and knew exactly what he liked, what he wanted. The car he had promised himself when still a kid. The one he would buy when he grew up.

* * *

Ben recalled the moment he first saw it, on a detested family holiday on the Norfolk coast. Living in a tent on a grim campsite under perpetually leaden skies. Ben had hated that holiday where it had seemed to rain every single day. Ben loathed camping and never received a satisfactory response from his parents when he asked why they couldn't stay in a hotel, like other people.

He had hated the patches of dead yellow grass, giant urine stains left behind by departed campers. He had hated having no one to play with, or at least someone to share his misery. He had hated having to sleep in a sweaty nylon sleeping bag on a camp bed. The stupid tent's distorting plastic windows pretending to be real ones. The stupid spindly camping stove balanced precariously on uneven ground. The stacking saucepans with their folding handles and, at night, the overpowering smell of burning paraffin in his nostrils from the lamp that had to be primed first and then made a horrible hissing noise, a siren call to a squadron of demented flying bugs.

But worse than this. The worst thing by far. The thing he had hated most was the horror that was the communal ablutions block.

* * *

It was an ugly low-rise concrete building a hundred and fifty yards distant. Separate entrances for men and women. Twin rows of cracked rust-stained hand basins down the middle, rumbling, shuddering pipes. Toilets, some with missing door locks. Obscene graffiti in indelible felt pen. Shower stalls with limp, mildewed curtains.

Ben still trembled when he remembered the dark evenings. Shivering and stumbling across damp grass in pyjamas too short in arm and leg. The scratchy blue dressing gown with the gold piping. How he had clutched his wash bag in one hand, a towel draped over his arm, and a rubberised torch with a dodgy switch and slowly dying yellow light in the other.

How he had waved it around ineffectively trying to pick out tent pegs and guy ropes laying in wait for him in the gloom, tripwires which he imagined would trigger floodlights in a rapid series of heavy clunks all around the campsite, blinding him in their glare, paralysing him with fear. Snarling yellow-eyed guard dogs released from their pens, all fangs and lolling tongues dripping with rabid saliva charging towards him, trained to rip him limb from limb. It was on this holiday that a shocking new realisation dawned on Ben: he had begun to hate his parents.

* * *

Primarily, however, he remembered the holiday as the first time he saw the two-seater open top sports car in that outrageously flamboyant turquoise colour, turning his hitherto monochrome life technicolour.

Ben had been with his parents, as always, sitting outside in the beer garden of a Royal Oak, or a White Swan, he couldn't remember, it didn't matter. They were having lunch. He heard it before he saw it, Ben's ears pricking up at the glorious rumble of the engine coming from the road, just beyond the hedge, the noise getting louder but the source remaining indeterminate. Then it revealed itself, rounded the corner of the pub and drove across the virtually empty car park, tyres spitting out tiny stones, scrunching across the gravel and skidding to a halt with a final rev of the engine.

All three of them, Ben and his parents, turned as one to look. Seeking the cause of this disturbance. Their looks turning into stares, when an impossibly glamorous couple (at least in Ben's eyes), a man and a much younger woman, climbed out of the car. They didn't bother about putting the roof up, or even locking the doors. They just carelessly abandoned this fantastic machine right there in the car park. The young woman was pretty and had laughed easily at some unheard joke. She was tidying her windswept blonde hair as the man, shorter than she, came around the side of the car, put an arm around her waist and together they noisily swept into the pub, as though they owned it. Ben, sat there at the trestle table in the overcast garden had muttered under his breath, 'I bet *they* don't stay on campsites.'

The commotion caused by the arrival of the glamorous couple could not be ignored, contrasting, as it did, so dramatically with the quiet desperation exuded by Ben's parents. Until this point, Ben's parents had been sitting in silence, there being nothing left to say once they had decided upon their food and drink order: a glass of dry white wine, large, for her, a pint of bitter, Tetley's, for him. Ben had said he wanted a Coca Cola, no lemon, and his mother had asked for the magic word and given him that look when he replied.

"Er… Abracadabra?"

And three ploughman's lunches. But now, for some reason, Ben's parents began to make derisive comments about the very people who had just livened everything up.

What surprised Ben most was that it was his father who had started it, nodding in the direction of the pub doorway, making remarks about the appearance of the driver: his lack of height (Ben's father was relatively tall); his bald head (his father had a full head of hair); the belly overhanging ludicrously checked shorts (his father was whippet thin); the ankle socks and sandals. Oddly, he didn't mention the car at all, or the pretty young girl who may, or may not, have been his niece. Anyway, the couple had seemed very happy together, clearly having fun. Could it be that his father was jealous?

Then it was Ben's mother's turn. She had that tight-lipped expression Ben knew so well, and she seemed to be a bit short with his father. She said something about a 'dolly bird' but by then Ben was no longer listening, he was more interested in the car. He wandered over to it, the still warm engine making ticking noises. Ben walked around it at a respectful distance, inspecting it from all angles: noting the low-slung body, the long smooth bonnet, the shiny eight-hole wheels. He approached a bit nearer, peering inside at the leather seats, the dials, the switches, all those buttons to play with. It was a Mercedes Benz, Ben knew that from the three-pointed star set into the radiator grill, and the chrome badge on the boot lid told him it was a '500 SL'. It was nothing like their little white Peugeot. Ben's reverie was broken by his father's voice.

"Come away from there son."

★ ★ ★

Ben had done his research, the quest had taken time, had demanded uncompromising patience, but he finally found one. The exact model. The right colour; the rare two-tone teal blue, the turquoise metallic. An SL with a V8 engine. Built when cars were designed by engineers not accountants. Low mileage too. Ben had problems finding an insurer and ended up paying a ridiculous premium, but he didn't care. It was worth it.

- V -

Ben meets Louise

Ben was in a good mood. He bounded into the organic teahouse. In a couple of days he would collect his sports car. A whole summer of open top driving lay ahead of him, his arm casually, invitingly, draped over the backrest of the vacant passenger seat.

On the way in he noted that his favoured chair, the red leather wing back in the window was vacant. He strode up confidently to the counter and ordered a Midnight Grey from the young woman dressed in a thin white singlet bearing the slogan, 'Add me to your wish list', her denim shorts so skimpy that white pockets stuck out over blue tights printed with large images of kittens. There was the flash of a gold tooth when she spoke.

Typical Ben, he was working his way systematically through the black teas. Though he thought he might give the 'Caramel sweetheart' a miss, and was not at all sure about the 'Walk in the Wood'. But he definitely intended to move into the uncharted boiled waters of the green ones in due course. Waiting for his tea, Ben considered pretending to stifle a sneeze over the assorted array of cakes before him, but decided against it.

★ ★ ★

Ben collected his tea on a tray from a sustainable source and carefully rounded the thick column in the middle of the room, aiming towards his chair, only to see that his chair was now occupied. A woman. He pulled up. Where had she come from? Miffed, but not sufficiently to spoil his good mood, he steered his tray towards the vacant two-seater sofa opposite her. At least he was by the window, and maybe this woman would leave and he could quickly swap seats. Ben placed his tray on the low table, pulled the bag across his shoulder up over his head, and took out his laptop. Firing it up to take advantage of the free Wi-Fi.

While his computer was booting up, Ben stole a glance at the interloper opposite. The cuckoo in his nest, twin-thumb texting away at a ridiculous velocity, and found he was unable to drag his eyes back to the screen now patiently requesting the teahouse's password. He was staring, he knew he shouldn't, but was powerless. His eyes magnetised. He didn't want her to catch him, but he couldn't look away either. She was gorgeous. Unlike most of his friends, who tended to concentrate on primary and secondary sexual characteristics, Ben was attracted by the face first, and was immediately drawn to the deep twin vertical tramlines that appeared in the middle of her forehead as she concentrated fixedly on her phone. Then he noticed the dark, flashing eyes in the pale, high cheek-boned face, a face framed by slightly tangled shoulder-length dark hair (bed hair?). Then he took in the bottle green short-sleeved t-shirt – the colour really suited her. She was small-boned, could probably shop at Baby Gap opposite (not really). She looked almost fragile with her pale, thin, almost twig-like arms, but at the same time he sensed she possessed a powerful inner strength. He wouldn't want to cross her. Who was she texting so furiously? Her boyfriend probably.

Something chemical, something electrical was occurring in Ben's synapses. She moved in her seat and he was sure he could definitely make out nipples as her small rounded breasts pressed against the cotton fabric. Was she wearing a bra? He was reminded that a male friend once assured him that there was absolutely no question about it, women knew exactly what they were doing with their breasts, at all times. The same friend who made the observation that girls' bikini bottoms always rode up the right buttock cheek, never the left. The charmer, reknowned for not beating around the bush, who sagely noted that, unlike men who played the percentages, women hate being rejected because, at the end of the day it was simple, 'Women, love, cock.'

Ben was not entertaining such base thoughts as he surveyed the vision opposite wearing a long ankle-length mauve skirt, and something Ben hadn't seen before, black ankle-height Dr Martin boots, with a 3-inch rubber heel. Moving back up, he noted ring-less fingers; a simple pink coral necklace; and large hoop earrings with one smaller one, a sleeper, higher up, pierced through the cartilage of the helix. No discernable make-up. Ben disliked obvious signs of make-up: surely the purpose of which was to disguise perceived flaws, not be an end in itself, where all you can think of is what does she really look like under all that slap, and what further levels of deception were being perpetrated to try and attract the poor simple creature that is the male of the species?

★ ★ ★

Gorgeous. No, she was more than that, after all there were a lot of gorgeous women out there. You noticed them all the time: a long mane of hair, hair tied up with yet more hair; a casual toss of the head; an effortlessly tied scarf; a glance, a flash of the eye; a smile; a sensuous mouth; a skin tone; a languorous, feline deportment; a whiff of perfume; a shapely, swaying arse in tight denim, legs tapering into brown leather boots...

This one looked gorgeous all right, but there was something else about her. She looked interesting. She intrigued him. That was it. He wanted to get to know her, not just admire her. He wanted to talk to her, reveal himself to her, make her respond, encourage (not humour) him. That thing with Gnat was over.

45

Ben was ready, more than ready, for something more…
engaging.

He decided he had to get to know her, could not
let her escape. But how? The question invaded and
conquered all other thoughts. Everything else, the
unopened e-mails, the new car, all relegated, kicked
into the long grass of his mind.

★ ★ ★

Ben caught her eye for that tiny, immeasurable fraction
of a second longer than usual. Had he imagined it? On
the tube you sit directly opposite other human beings
in a closely confined place. No possible flight until the
next station, but that's okay, they're normal people,
right? The people alongside you, opposite you. Regular
people, just like you, just a bit different, that's all. But
the unwritten rule, tube etiquette, dictated that you
never ever make direct eye contact. If by accident this
should happen, then you both look away immediately,
like it never happened.

On the tube you become adept using peripheral
vision, automatically categorising, filing away
your fellow passengers when they weren't looking
at you, or had their heads down, reading, doing
sudoku, playing games on their phones. If you did
get caught, you immediately pretended you were
studying the underground map, or reading the
terrible advertisements over their heads. Adverts for
hair loss treatments, anti-ageing creams, and travel

insurance. The only permissible exceptions to this rule are when you want to borrow another passenger's just-discarded free newspaper, or the driver comes on with an announcement of a delay or, less likely, a witty comment which might, just might, provoke an involuntary acknowledgement within the carriage. The raising of an eyebrow perhaps, or a barely perceptible nod of the head to a fellow passenger before going on to ignore them for the rest of the journey.

★ ★ ★

This was different. They had made eye contact, and he wanted to take things further. He wanted to engage her in conversation, but what should he say, what could he, say? You simply don't talk to strangers in London unless you're inebriated. Would she think him a creep? Ignore him? Move away? He remembered 'Sliding Doors', a film with that annoyingly winsome actress now 'uncoupled' or something to the guy in that awful band of serial bedwetters, the whole future course of her life determined by which tube train she catches. This could be his 'sliding doors' moment. He may never see her again. He had to summon the courage. He had to say something. Then it came to him.

★ ★ ★

Ben put his cup down in the saucer, a little clumsily, a little too noisily. He then snapped shut the lid of his laptop with a sigh and looked up directly at the gorgeous creature. In the most casual, most unlike 'loony on the bus' voice he could muster, he asked her a question.

"Excuse me, do you know what happened to the pet shop that used to be here? Do you know what happened to the talking monkeys?"

Ben realised, too late, that he had meant to say parrots, but she didn't seem to notice. She smiled at him. Was that almost a laugh he thought? She responded. She had a very proper voice.

"I don't know. I only ever visited once. I remember being terrified by the spiders. They were climbing up the sides of the glass tanks. I thought they would escape. Tarantulas and other huge, hairy... arachnids."

Louise held his gaze.

Ben thought 'arachnids?' Only David Attenborough, Sir David Attenborough, ever called spiders arachnids. He suddenly doubted himself. Was he out of his depth? Was she too good for him? What had he been thinking? Ben was momentarily flummoxed. He needed to recover quickly, say something. Come up with a suitable rejoinder. Follow through, do something. But nothing was coming. He decided to try and buy some time. He knew it was a cop out, he was playing his cards too soon, but it was all he could think of.

Lifting himself from the sofa, grabbing at the laptop as it slid towards the floor, he leant over the ridiculously low, ridiculously wide table dividing them and stretched out a hand.

"Hi, I'm Ben."

The gorgeous woman, her smile transformed into a sheepish grin, half rose herself, and with a gracious, slightly downward and sideward turn of the head, extended her own hand, palm down, as if he was expected to kiss it. And he did. He had no idea why. Had no idea what came over him. It was pure reflex. He had bent even lower over the table and raised the back of Louise's hand to his lips.

Looking back, Ben remembered the image that had flashed through his head, a scene from a previous life, in Prussia. No, the Austro-Hungarian court: an orchestra striking up anew with a Strauss waltz. An extravagantly moustachioed man in formal military attire, medals flashing on a barrel chest. A duelling scar, a small nick on his cheek, bowing down gracefully to enquire whether the seated lady, all heaving bosoms constrictively laced into a bodice, clothing permitting only shallow breaths, breaths channelled necessarily upwards (hence the heaving), a carefully arranged bustle, the train splayed out around her, probably waving a fan. And the officer asking her whether she would give him the pleasure.

"And I'm Louise."

Both sat back again, Louise wearing a bemused, expression, thinking, 'What now?' And Ben thinking, 'Zoologist'. That's it. She must work at the zoo.

"Do you work at the zoo?"

Louise was puzzled. An odd thing to say.

"Why do you ask that?"

"Arachnids. You said arachnids."

"Oh! No, no. No. I'm a teacher. I'm a teacher with a phobia about spiders. You know, arachnophobia?"

"Ah."

Ben noticed Louise had finished her drink (what had it been?) but was making no move to leave. But she might, any minute he thought, panicking slightly. He didn't want her to go. Then he had another brainwave. He pointed to her empty cup.

"Would you like another cup of…?"

"Tea? Yes, that would be lovely, Midnight Grey, thank you."

She's drinking the same as me thought Ben, realising immediately how dim-witted it would sound to point this out.

★ ★ ★

What Ben didn't realise however, not until Louise informed him later, what he had no way of knowing and, to be honest, had never given much thought to, was that Louise had already checked him out. A Darwinian reflex perhaps. An instinctive threat/suitability assessment. Whatever. Women were more attuned to their surroundings, aware of those around them: men, obviously, but women too, aka the competition. Other women even more so.

Within a matter of seconds of his approach, almost before he had sat down, without Ben having the faintest clue, Louise had processed the *de visu* intelligence gathered in one sweeping look, just like on the tube:

he was cute. He looked *agréable* (Ben would soon learn that Louise had a *penchant* for deploying French words even though there was a perfectly good English one available, unlike, say, well for *'penchant'* for example, or *'de visu'* (or was that Latin, yes? No? Dunno.) Ok, *'déjà vu'* then, or *'baguette'*. Nice hair, clean. He wasn't too tall. There was something about his eyes. She had taken in the polished brown penny loafers, the jeans, the pink shirt with just the lower buttons done up, the rolled up sleeves, a grey t-shirt underneath bearing a slogan – she could make out the letters 'EW YO'. New York? Louise had loved New York. The handsome plain, white-faced watch with the brown leather strap. The clipped, clean fingernails. The unadorned third finger of his left hand. She didn't like the bag though, too courier-ish.

* * *

Ben put his laptop aside on the small sofa, entrusting it to Louise, and leapt up to go back to the counter to place a new order with the girl in the singlet. Looking back over his shoulder at the gorgeous creature now known as Louise, sitting there, head down, in his seat. Ben thought to himself that he didn't just want to add Louise to his 'wish list', he wanted to put her in his basket, proceed straight to checkout and click same day delivery. This is going very well he thought.

Meanwhile Louise, her eyes having followed his retreating form, looked away. She wondered if she had made a mistake. Had she been too quick to accept his offer? She was having doubts. Might he think she was some crazy bitch, some 'bunny boiler' who sat around all day waiting to be chatted up by strangers? What if he was a psycho? She would be stuck with him now while she drank the tea, the tea he was buying her, letting him think that she now owed him. He might follow her out. She should have refused his offer, just stayed there until she could make a better-informed judgement. All these thoughts passed through her head until she saw him heading back towards her, bearing a tray, just for her, his eyes shining and a huge warm smile on his face. She beamed back up at him.

- VI -

Louise

Louise did not have any tattoos, nor did she have facial hair but, as Ben had observed, she did have pierced ears. It would be a short while, however, before Ben discovered to his surprise, and their shared erotic delight, that Louise had a further piercing. But this one was in a private place and so far only two other people were aware of it, or had ever seen it. Shane was one, obviously, and Vicky, Louise's best friend was the other.

* * *

Vicky had gone with her, to lend moral support she said, but with an undeniable prurience whilst, at the same time, not believing Louise would actually go through with it. They had clomped up the wooden stairs together, Vicky following Louise, into the 'Tattoo and Piercing Studio' above the leather goods shop on Chalk Farm Road, right next door to the Electric Ballroom.

The place where, with a nonchalance she did not feel, Louise disappeared behind a partition to sit on a low couch covered with a paper towel unspooled from a giant roll fixed on a stand at one end. Where she unzipped and removed knee-high boots before standing, once again, to reach up under her short tartan skirt to roll down thick black tights. All in the presence of a gentle, softly-spoken guy in a faded t-shirt which did nothing to hide, in fact, only served to emphasise his protruding belly. A guy with receding hair drawn tightly back from his face in a lank ponytail, ornate tattooed sleeves on both his arms and a silver ring through his nose. Shane.

* * *

If she were honest, Louise felt slighted, disappointed, desexualised even. Shane, a man, was standing right there in front of her, disinterested, complete indifference as she sat down again and slowly, deliberately, removed the last vestige of her modesty, the last line of defence. He ignored her, busying himself instead with pulling on surgical gloves, that unmistakable sucking, smacking sound, and now fitting a sterilised 3.5mm surgical steel ball closure ring into a piercing gun.

Shane had been unfazed by Louise's request. In over fifteen years of inking and piercing he had heard, seen, and done it all. When Louise explained what she wanted, he simply nodded, his ponytail bouncing beyond his shoulder. The only proviso, before Louise fished in her bag and produced payment in advance, was that he wouldn't be able to do it if Louise was having her period: there would be a risk of infection, see? Louise assured him it was fine.

Louise lay back on the couch and shifted herself to give Shane a precise indication as to where she wanted it, not sure if Shane knew his way around. Shane sank onto his stool which let out a pneumatic sigh, he leant forward, right over her, so close. He gently pulled at a sticky *labium minus* with the latexed thumb and forefinger of one hand and, with the other, pressed his gun against soft flesh and fired.

It was all over in a matter of seconds. Louise said it hadn't hurt at all, and shortly afterwards both were excitedly and noisily clambering back down the stairs, just like in the schoolgirl adventures they had once shared, except this time Louise's tights were stuffed into her handbag, and in her other hand she clutched a leaflet with advice on care and hygiene during the healing process.

They headed straight for the pub at the lock on the canal, spirited by the outrageousness of it all, and in need of a drink.

- VII -

More Louise

At twenty-five, Louise was three years younger than Ben and, like him, an only child. She had been christened Mary-Louise, but ever since she could remember had loathed the implied religiosity of the name Mary. Louise's disdain could be traced directly back to the weekly Confirmation classes she was forced to endure as a child. Classes that ruined her Sunday mornings and filled her with dread and incredulity in equal measure.

Louise had had to walk the half mile to the church, each step taking her closer to the hypodermic steeple dominating the horizon. An implied threat to inject you if you refused to take the jowly vicar with the red-veined nose seriously. Inject you like that time at school when they all had to line up in their vests for the, no getting out of it, vaccination that left your arm numb and you couldn't do netball or rounders the next day.

* * *

At age eleven, Louise was congenitally unable to sit still. Congregated in the northern transept of that bone grey church alongide a handful of other children, equally bored and impatient, she fidgeted constantly on the unforgiving pew, her legs swinging in the air. Louise's abiding memory was the cold, of feeling cold, even on the sunniest of days.

Before entering the cavernous gloom of the church, Louise remembered having to pick her way through stone tombs, edifices taller than she, inscriptions no longer legible but with cracks large enough for ghouls and other phantasmagoria to flit in and out at will. Louise felt sure, if you dared to stop and peer into them, you'd see luminous skulls and bones picked out against a malevolent blackness.

But Louise didn't stop. She would hum to herself for protection. She would skip past the ancient sarcophagi, the headstones like crooked teeth in need of serious orthodontics, and into the church that her parents only ever attended once or, max, twice a year, but which she had to go to every week. It was all so unfair!

★ ★ ★

The Vicar would stand there weaving ridiculous stories they were expected to accept as gospel, and make confounding references to a 'holy ghost'. A *holy ghost*? Louise had looked it up in her Concise English Dictionary: holy *a. & n. 1. a. Consecrated, sacred; morally*

*and spiritually perfect; belonging to, empowered by, devoted
to God; of high moral excellence; (in trivial excl.: holy cow!
holy mackerel! holy smoke.*) And then she had looked up
ghost, just to make sure she wasn't missing anything:
ghost – *n. Soul of a dead person in Hades etc; spectre esp. of
dead person appearing to be living.* Hades *(-z) n. (Gk Myth.)
lower world, abode of departing spirits; (euphem.) = hell 2. [f.
Gk haides (orig. a name of Pluto), transl. Heb…*

Louise gave up.

★ ★ ★

Sometimes she would just drift off, enter into the
brightly hued painting hanging high up on the wall, a
gilt-framed reproduction, a pre-Renaissance depiction
of Jesus, arms outstretched in welcome. He looked hot
she thought, McDreamy. She liked his long hair, and
those piercing blue eyes that would seek her out each
week, no matter where she sat. She knew of course,
everyone knew, that Jesus was born in Bethlehem two
thousand years ago ('Oh Little Town of Bethlehem'…
Anno Domini) and raised on the West Bank (Jesus of
Nazareth, right?). Now Louise was learning that, as a
young man, Jesus decided he had a calling: his destiny
was not to follow in the footsteps of his "father" and
the life of a small town carpenter turning out roughly-
hewn chairs, tables, and shelving. Jesus had been
chosen. He had received clear instructions from an
Angel. He had been charged with a sacred undertaking:
a message people needed to hear if they were to save

themselves. They needed to know that there would be a day of reckoning, a day of judgement, and that they needed to change their ways, for this day was imminent.

Louise was taught that Jesus reinvented himself as a prophet, a 'holy man'. In truth not such an unusual career choice back in those days when superstition and ignorance were rife. Jesus left home, bidding his tearful, uncomprehending parents farewell. Parents who, until their dying day questioned where they had gone wrong. How Jesus had got mixed up in the wrong crowd. How and when had he been radicalised. Who had planted all those fanciful ideas in his head? And why oh why hadn't they spotted the warning signs? That halo?

Jesus went away leaving Mary and Joseph clinging to the hope that it was just a phase. That he was just taking a gap year. That he would soon return to his rightful place, alongside his father, continue his apprenticeship in the lean-to workshop next door.

★ ★ ★

Jesus had travelled overland to Galilee and Samaria. But in the course of discovering himself, he discovered he was not alone: he was just one of many prophets on the circuit. Jesus needed a gimmick, a USP.

Bingo! He would become a *raconteur*. Jesus came up with the idea of parables. He began narrating stories to get his message over. Stories ordinary hard working people could relate to. He began to carve out a career for himself (short-lived it transpired), but there was more, and this was what clinched it, what truly set him apart: to illustrate the stories, get this, HE would perform magic tricks. Genius!

Jesus began to cause quite a stir. Through talent, charisma, and word of mouth, he was building up quite a fanbase. From far and wide, more and more people gathered to listen to his stories and watch the show. But then it began to go to his head. Jesus got carried away when a dozen or so, twelve of his hardcore fans, began touting him as God's progeny and he did nothing to dispel the notion. Only at the very end of his life did he give himself away when publicly, and somewhat embarrasingly, he betrayed doubts to his pious followers.

The Romans didn't give a damn. They had their own gods. But the Jewish religious establishment could not tolerate Jesus any longer. They'd had enough of the unorthodox teachings of this uneducated upstart villager, this *Shmegegge,* and it was ultimately Jesus's hubris that proved to be his downfall.

Louise concluded something along these lines.

* * *

There was more. Louise could not help noticing that the image of Jesus conjured up by the vicar was distinctly at odds with the one hanging on the wall. In the painting, Jesus was a Caucasian male with film star looks. He was dressed in mediaeval European clothing. Furthermore, for some reason, the painting featured the flag of St George. Louise had no idea that St George had been a Roman soldier in Cappadocia in the 3rd century AD, note *AD*, but she did sense something did not quite add up.

It made even less sense when Louise's study of the picture appeared to contradict what the vicar was saying, when she focused on the castle in the background (or what should have been the background – but this being *pre*-Renaissance, of course, artists had yet to get a handle on perspective), and horse-mounted soldiers in chain mail, brandishing lances, and not-to-scale hunting dogs running around. Louise had assumed the castle to be contemporaneous with the life of Jesus, and it would be several years later, in a History class, before she learned that the first castle to appear in Galilee was built by the Crusaders as part of the war effort defending the Holy Land from the Musselman, i.e. 1600 years *after* Jesus had died on the cross. Or had he? Had he been pretending? Had this been another one of his magic tricks? Even this was no longer clear to Louise.

After one Confirmation class, Louise had found herself more baffled than usual but, unlike at school, she did not raise her hand to seek clarification, intuiting correctly that the vicar would be annoyed. Anyway, as she had no wish to prolong the class she tried to work the confusion out in her head: Mary Carpenter/Mary Magdalene. It was not always clear who was who in the stories. The virgin, the mother, the prostitute. If you're a virgin you can't have a baby. Louise knew that. And hadn't she heard that the word 'virgin' had been a mistranslation from the original Aramaic? And if Joseph wasn't the father, then maybe she was a prostitute, and Gabriel was no Angel.

It went on in Louise's head. Could you be a virgin and a prostitute? Well yes, Louise supposed, if it was your first time, or if you didn't go 'all the way'. But all she really knew was that she didn't like the name Mary. She just wanted the class to be over so she could get back out into the sunshine, go home.

- VIII -

Yet more Louise

When Louise went away to Manchester to study Eng. Lit., she ditched 'Mary' completely. She became simply 'Louise', romantically identifying herself with the character in an eponymously-titled '80s song by The Human League. Her father still called her Marylou, as did Vicky, but Louise's relationship with her mother, increasingly distant as the years went by, meant she no longer appeared to address Louise by any name during the infrequent visits she made home. The long journey south on the train to Euston, then the Northern line to Waterloo where she would emerge to catch an overcrowded commuter train to her parents' house, set back behind a tall box hedge in 'One of West Byfleet's most sought after residential streets.'

★ ★ ★

It had seemed such a retrograde step. After Manchester. Moving back home. It just wasn't right. She was a grown up! But what else could she do? It would have been daft to spend what little money she was earning on renting a bedsit while completing her probation as a teaching assistant, a Year 3 class at the local state junior. It had been okay going home during uni holidays, but to return permanently, to the time capsule of her bedroom, where the only thing that had changed was her, had been awful.

She had enjoyed the freedom and responsibility of sharing that huge warren of a house in Fallowfield with her new mates (the area, no reflection on their intellectual acuity had been the joke), rooms divided with plywood party walls to increase student density and maximise rental income. Okay the area had been pretty grim, and she used to hide her laptop under her pillow because the houses were constantly being broken into, but they had had a pretty wild time, and she could share her bed whenever she liked with Mark, her first proper boyfriend. But now, every morning, she would find herself, once again, facing her mother over the breakfast table. Her mother who seemed to resent her presence, who always seemed to look at her sideways in a disapproving manner, who made critical comments about her clothes, the state of her hair or, even worse, the state of her room. And all this before Louise set off for the very same school she had attended as a pupil not so many years before. It had struck Louise that her life was turning out to be just too perverse to be true.

Evenings had been even worse. Over dinner, with her parents, Louise would find it increasingly difficult to tolerate her mother's blinkered world view, her sanctimonious, Daily Mail-like pharisaic hypocrisy. Louise's father had long since learned not to respond beyond the minimum he could get away with. Occasionally he and Louise would exchange conspiratorial glances when her mother was on one of her hobbyhorses. Once or twice they had been caught out and there had been hell to pay. Louise felt sorry for her mild-mannered dad. She knew he was proud of her. He was a good man, well liked, the CFO of a construction company. But sometimes, just sometimes, Louise would wish he would 'Man up', or 'Grow a pair', before remembering this was her father she was thinking about.

Then would come the interminable weekends. Whenever she could Louise would get away, but it wasn't always that easy, stuck out in Surrey, most of her friends spread around the country. After a year of this purgatory however, a year where she had worked hard and conscientiously, Louise became an NQT, a newly qualified teacher and, shortly thereafter, experienced one of the most thrilling moments of her life so far when she learned she had landed a job in a small Prep school in Hampstead. Her adult life could finally begin: she would move to central London and join Vicky who was already there. They would share a flat together, just as they had always dreamed they would, back in the dorm.

* * *

Louise and Vicky's friendship dated from their school days when Louise, 'the Locust' – a sobriquet earned due an uncanny ability to eat copious quantities of school food without any discernable effect – had stood up for Vicky when the other girls were being unkind about her body shape. Vicky was on the large size, there was no denying: the first in their small gang to menstruate, the first to wear a 'training' bra (mortifyingly revealed in the changing room at the start of term), when the joke became Vicky was training for the 'Tit Olympics', and all agreed that Louise was never, ever, likely to qualify, let alone attain podium, and Louise feeling secretly relieved.

* * *

Louise and Vicky had moved in together, renting a small two-bedroomed Victorian conversion in Kentish Town. Vicky had turned out to be arty, and not untalented. After graduating art college she landed a job as a graphic designer on a trashy weekly gossip magazine. It seemed glamorous at the time and, to a degree, it still was. It paid reasonably well and she got invited to a few parties and promo events. It allowed her to feel as though she was on some sort of inside track, but the artist inside her suspected that the job was slightly demeaning, and she had recently confided to Louise that she might start looking to move on.

For Louise, it was just a short bus ride up the hill to her new school. She loved the old-fashioned red brick building with the steep gables. She loved the cute uniforms: silver-trimmed navy blazers, short grey trousers and caps for the boys. Long blue and white-striped shift dresses, straw hats with ribbons for the girls. Foreign tourists visiting Hampstead would stop, take out their phones and take pictures of these 'typical' British school children. One time Louise had witnessed a group of Italian tourists pointing at the children and shouting, *'Foto, foto!'* Louise had laughed out loud and felt proud when the kids, *mes enfants*, just ran away, did a starburst, disappearing down the narrow alleyways.

She got on well with most of her colleagues, apart from Peter, the deputy Head with the sinister wire-framed glasses. She thought him creepy and completely lacking in self-awareness as he continued to make crude passes at her.

She wasn't too fond of the autocratic headmaster and owner either, nor his overbearing wife, a matronly figure who, despite having no teaching qualifications whatsoever, insisted on taking classes whenever the mood took her. The Head's daughter, in the Third Grade, was undeniably bright, but spoilt. With her blonde hair teased into ringlets and a chubby face, she looked like Shirley Temple, but with a permanent frown. Indeed, all the teachers referred to her as Shirley to avoid being overheard criticizing the precocious daughter as they exchanged tales of her latest bullying antics in the classroom, or the playground. All the teachers, including Louise (to her newly qualified, idealistic shame) overlooked or downplayed Shirley's behaviour. Nobody wanted Shirley going home and complaining to her parents about the 'Horrible, nasty teacher'.

Otherwise, Louise was very happy. The kids were nice and, unlike some at her old school, this lot were all like little sponges. Keen to demonstrate their grasp of the teachings, to bask in the teacher's praise. Louise was loving it, and the children adored her.

★ ★ ★

When not working, Louise and Vicky found they spent most of their time at home, playing music, cooking, laughing. London was expensive. The flat had a large bathroom where they would spend hours doing manipeds and depilation. But at weekends, they went out. Mostly in neighbouring Camden Town where they would explore the Stables market, the former home for the horses that once pulled barges along the canal. Here they would browse the 'vintage' clothes stalls and eat delicious Asian food standing up. Food served on polystyrene plates with plastic forks. Surrounded by Asian voices shouting out their dishes, vying for attention as though in a Thai street market. Or they would just hang out in the pubs and cafes, lingering over bottled beer or skinny lattes. Once a week was cinema night. They would go to the Odeon on Parkway, sit low in their seats and devour frozen fruit yoghurt ice creams. Occasionally they would score some weed from the dudes impudently hanging around in full view of the CCTV cameras in Inverness Street. They would then return home to share inexpertly rolled joints, the TV tuned to a late night shopping channel which would reduce them to tear-streaming laughter, and the intense citron-*icity* of a lemon cheesecake from the fridge would blow their minds.

* * *

On at least one such evening, probably two – Louise's memory was a bit hazy, possibly deliberately – they had found themselves kissing, demonstrating different techniques. It started out as a joke but lead to them comforting each other in the same bed, giggling under the covers. It was a bit weird at first, but the THC, the tetrahydrocannabinol, removed any inhibitions they may otherwise have had, and the heightened sense of taste and touch had felt pretty good. And, after all, they were best friends. When they awoke to daylight, still a bit groggy, they had simply untangled themselves, got up and carried on as normal. One would put the kettle on; the other would stack the dishwasher. They never referred to these occasions. What was there to say? Neither were they embarrassed. They weren't lesbians. They didn't consider themselves to be bisexual either: they both liked boys, but there hadn't been any around.

Vicky idolised Louise and always strove to cheer her up if Louise should come home upset – some nonsense in the staff room perhaps. Vicky also had a nice line in self-deprecation which she knew Louise enjoyed because it offered Louise a chance to reciprocate. One evening Vicky had returned to the flat with her dark hair freshly bobbed and sporting a fringe which didn't do her any favours. Vicky had regarded herself in the mirror in the hallway, Louise standing next to her. Vicky let her shoulders droop and, her face like a dropped pie, sighed.

"Shit. I've turned into Dawn French. And not in a good way."

Louise had smiled a sorority smile back at Vicky in the mirror, kissed her on the shoulder and squeezed her hand.

* * *

Both Louise and Vicky's online status (or according to Louise, as the word was a Latin fourth declension noun, 'statuses' was also permissible) were currently unattached. In fact, discounting any sex acts performed with Vicky, which didn't count, Louise had not had sex for nearly a year, not since moving back to her parents. Vicky, on the other hand, who had developed a Rubenesque voluptuousness was not quite as selective as she might have been, especially after a few drinks.

Since moving in together at the beginning of the year, Vicky had brought back several guys to the flat. She reckoned it was safer to bring them home, with Louise likely to be around, than to risk going back to his place. And the guys had proved more than happy to do this as they could then leave whenever they wanted. None of that awkward stuff in the morning. Just leave with a promise to call.

Sometimes Vicky would shamelessly try to scandalise or embarrass Louise, and Louise would pretend not to listen, not to hear. Sometimes even going so far as to stick her fingers in her ears and go, 'La, la, lalaa, lalalaaaaalalaaa!' As Vicky attempted to give a blow by blow account of her conquests, often in cruel, graphic detail. Like that time with the guy with a penis like a walnut whip, 'Minus the walnut'. Or the huge guy who was so proud of himself yet completely unable to maintain an erection. Or the exhibitionist Vicky sent naked into the kitchen one time, knowing Louise was there, telling him to propose that she come and join them in a threesome.

In response to these provocations, Louise teased Vicky that if she was 'the Locust', then Vicky was 'the Black Widow', a venomous spider with an hour-glass figure and twice the size of the male of the species. Notwithstanding her arachnophobia, Louise had Googled it and read out how, after mating, the Black Widow 'Uses her exoskeleton to crush the male and puncture him with her *chelicerae*, thereby allowing the administration of lethal digestive enzymes that liquefy the male body. The female then sucks up the resulting fluid, cannibalising her erstwhile mate.' Scrolling down, Louise revealed that the reason the Black Widow did this was because sex made her hungry, and he was there, spent, on a plate, as it were. Way too late, too late to stop, Louise realised that she had gone too far. This was not the action of a best friend. Louise got up and went around the table, over to Vicky, sitting opposite her in the kitchen. From behind Louise put her arms around Vicky and kissed the side of her neck. She told Vicky it was rubbish. She was nothing like a Black Widow.

- IX -

Ben and Louise

Louise was eulogising again.

"He's always positive. Enthusiastic. It's infectious! He reads a lot. He knows stuff."

Vicky agreed this was important.

"He's interesting. He has this, I don't know, zest for life. He sees things differently, has a different perspective. He questions where most just accept. And he really makes me laugh."

There was more.

"He's sexy. I like his clothes, the way he dresses, he's a bit of a hipster, *mais sans barbe.* When he looks at me, those eyes, it's like he's seeing right inside me, and I don't mind! He looks at me with a sort of… inquisitive hunger. It's strange, he makes me feel safe."

Louise looked directly at Vicky, laughing out loud.

"Does that sound stupid? Am I stupid?"

Vicky, apart from wondering, why she had never, ever told Louise that her occasional lapses into French were an *affectation absurde* (*'Mais sans barbe'* for fuck's sake!), responded with a vomiting gesture, two fingers down her throat, and then threw a cushion across the canyon dividing the two sofas of their shared living room. The cushion striking Louise smack in the face.

"He sounds like a total wanker to me."

Louise threw the cushion back half-heartedly, and Vicky batted it away dismissively. It fell to the floor where it remained, ignored, for the rest of the evening.

★ ★ ★

It had been almost four months since Ben and Louise met in the organic teahouse. Four whirlwind months during which they had fallen in love and told each other so. Louise saying it first: it had been early one morning, a refuse truck trundling down the street, iron gates thrown back on their hinges, black refuse sacks tossed into the jaws of the machine. They were in bed in Ben's flat. They had just made love. Ben still on top of her when she uttered those three little words. The three little words that are the biggest three little words in the whole world when you say them to someone for the very first time.

Nothing. Ben had said nothing. Just looked down at her intently, frowning. A look so intense that Louise became embarrassed. Nothing. Louise had squirmed... he was still inside her. Nothing. She had let out a nervous laugh, an attempt to play down this soul-bearing declaration that had left her feeling so emotionally exposed. Had she completely misread everything?

It wasn't that Ben didn't love her. He did. Oh, God, how he loved her! He just couldn't say it back like that. Not right there and then. Not just like that. It would sound crass: '*And I, love you, too-oo*'. Ben needed to tell her in his own time. On his own terms. Not carried away in an ecstatic moment. He needed to really mean it, to convey it with feeling, not just parrot the phrase back to her.

Ben did say it a little later that very same morning: he was bringing Louise a coffee made with his fancy new machine. There had almost been a tug of war as Ben, his thoughts consumed, neglected to release the small glass cup he was handing her. Then, *a propos* of nothing, he blurted out the same three little words Louise had uttered twenty minutes earlier but, despite himself, he bookended them with the very two words, the conjunction and the adverb he had desperately sought to avoid earlier. In Ben's head it was as though absolutely no time had elapsed since Louise had made her declaration.

"And I love you too."

- X -

Ben and Louise in love

Love at, sort of, first sight. It did happen. There was
such a thing. Ben and Louise were living proof. They
knew it. Even if they had only just told each other, they
had known it, really, ever since their first proper date, a
dinner in a smart yet funky Caribbean restaurant famed
for its curried goat. A place adrift amongst a sea of low
class run down establishments close to Camden Town
tube station. The restaurant where, for the first of many
evenings, they would gaze out at the street theatre from
the table in the window, the one set diagonally in the
corner, jammed in too close to the radiator. The table
where, on that first date, in a doomed attempt to defuse
a sexual tension incisable with a knife, a tension evident
not only to the attendant waiters and waitresses (and
subject of some ribald commentary), but other diners
too, tinged with varying degrees of jealousy. Where
Ben and Louise, probing and parrying, had exchanged
'witty' comments on the scene outside, on the names

of the stores and businesses opposite, and who might frequent the *Supa-save Convenience Store*; *The Blue Rose Licensed SEX Shop* where they wondered flirtatiously if *unlicensed* SEX shops existed, and how they might differ. *First Choice Kebabs; Fri Chicks* ('For when Mom's not cooking'); *Bang Bang Chicken* (BANG? Brilliant!'), *Booty Wine* (BOOTY??); and the *Classy Cutz Celebrity Salon* with its promise of 'uniSEX hair and beauty'.

They had planned to feel their way stealthily into this new relationship, but it was careering along, bearing them aloft. It was uncanny how much they appeared to have in common: shared likes and dislikes; views and opinions; families and childhood. It was becoming almost absurd, going so far as to lead both Ben and Louise to begin to suspect the other of nodding and agreeing out of politeness. An unwillingness to spoil the mood. They needn't have worried though as Ben discovered a hitherto unrealised fascination with the fulfillment to be gained imparting knowledge to minors. And Louise, well Louise had never been so interested in algorithms. It all seemed too good to be true.

* * *

In the first few weeks, there would follow many long evenings in this restaurant. Hours spent staring deep in each others shining eyes, talking, laughing, dreaming. Tactile exchanges across a table seemingly determined to keep them apart, they would feed each other, the suggestiveness of the act not lost on either of them, nor those looking on. More often than not they would be the last to leave, blissfully ignorant of the minimum wage staff lined up at the back of the room, arms folded, tired and with aching feet, wondering when they should break it up, not wanting to miss the next bus home, but at least assured of a generous tip from the regulars.

Evenings when they would carry on from where they had left off previously: gazing out the window, indulging in what had become a favourite pastime: making up empathetic stories about the lives of the transient, twilight inhabitants in the world outside their love bubble. The people at the bus stop for example, weighed down with shopping bags, sheltering from the drizzle. Waiting, forever waiting for the 29 to Wood Green, or the 134 to Kentish Town.

Then a double-decker would pull up, filling Ben and Louise's field of vision, forcing them back in their chairs, to adjust focus, before leaning forward once again to watch people jostle slyly, English-style, to board. Some struggling to maintain balance as they climbed the stairs to the top deck, one hand on the rail, the other trying to control the bags bashing against their legs as the bus lurched off, the driver, an impervious Buddha-like figure, immune behind a Perspex screen, wedged under an outsized steering wheel.

★ ★ ★

With the bus gone, the stop empty, Ben and Louise might then move on to speculate about the lives of those behind the grimy windows, greasy curtains and broken blinds of the Dickensian flats above the shops. Flats accessed through dusty doorways with haphazardly affixed buzzers and crude numerical and alphabetical annotations. Makeshift plywood doors you had to put a shoulder to in order to move the mountain of junk mail that would inevitably be piled up on the mat behind. Once inside, a steep staircase and a threadbare carpet would lead to over-furnished rooms with low-wattage, naked light bulbs. Ben and Louise felt very fortunate as they conjured up desperate domestic scenes, just like in a Walter Sickert painting. Sickert having been a leading light in the so-called 'Camden Town Group' of painters at the turn of the 20th Century.

* * *

Sleb spotting became another favourite pastime: a disproportionate number of actors, writers, musicians, and TV personalities lived in the area. Ben expressed to Louise his disappointment at not seeing a supermodel, known for her hard partying who, according to the Evening Standard, had been recently spotted sunbathing topless on Primrose Hill ('Really?', was Louise's sardonic response). Louise said she regretted the time she became tongue-tied when a famous actor said, 'After you' in the Whole Foods store, even though he was ahead of her in the queue. Both supermodel and actor members of a so-called Primrose Hill set, a group of people who had achieved notoriety in the tabloids – Vicky was the expert on this – for allegedly hedonistic lifestyles and a casual approach towards relationships.

* * *

Both fans of her music, it was perhaps surprising that neither Ben nor Louise had ever seen poor Amy. And now they never would, though Ben knew someone who claimed to have known her, someone who was keen to share his possibly apocryphal 'Wino' anecdotes with anyone who would care to listen, along with those who didn't.

Louise had seen one or her favourite authors though, the Liverpudlian Beryl Bainbridge. She too had died recently, though not in tragic circumstances like poor Amy. Louise said she had seen Beryl, hunched over, fag in hand, scuttling along Albert Street like a beetle (Ben: 'John, Paul, George, Ringo and Beryl, the fifth Beatle?').

* * *

Ben and Louise were really getting along. They discovered, and developed a shared interest in local history. Early on, in a shop on the Chalk Farm Road, there had been a slightly awkward moment when they came across a map of London dating from 1851, drawn in 3D from a hot air balloon tethered over Hampstead.

They decided they had to have it, but who exactly was buying it? And where would they hang it?

Louise taught Ben about Charles Dickens' association with the area and how, in Dombey & Son, he had written about the coming of the London and Birmingham Railway to Camden, and that he had lived in Bayham Street. His family moving there when his father was released from Marshalsea, the debtors' Prison. Charles's mother and his younger siblings had lived with his father actually in the prison, as was the custom back then – see Little Dorrit – but Charles, at 12, still a child himself, had lodged with a family friend in nearby College Street, and it was from there that he had walked each day to the factory, on the river near Charing Cross, where he would spend ten hours a day pasting labels onto jars of boot blacking before walking home again – see David Copperfield.

* * *

Ben shared with Louise his fascination with Emily Dimmock, the victim of the notorious 'Camden Town murder' in 1907, telling her that Sickert himself had been a prime suspect because he used local prostitutes as models, and that there had even been a highly imaginative link to Jack 'the Ripper'. Emily, it turned out, had followed the fate of many poor working class girls at the time, descending from domestic service into prostitution as a new era of mass transportation was ushered in, allowing illicit liaisons to flourish yet remain concealed.

Emily had been living in rented rooms with her partner, Bert (Ben: 'Note partner, not husband', Louise: *'tres progresive'*), but life had not been easy for hard working people in those days. Sacrifices had to be made, and accepting the fact that your wife, or partner in this case, could sell her body for some extra cash in times of need was justifiable. Indeed, one of Sickert's best known paintings was titled *'What shall we do for the rent?'* An unflattering portrait of a woman lying naked on a bed (Louise: 'You can clearly see his influence on Lucien Freud'), her head turned towards the wall, the presumed husband at the foot of the bed in waistcoat and shirtsleeves, head bowed, wringing his hands.

Ben said that Emily's body had been discovered in her bedroom. Her throat cut from ear to ear, the head almost severed. The police investigation revealed that Emily and Bert had been living beyond the means afforded by Bert's job on the railway, and that Bert had a cast iron alibi – he had been in Birmingham, at the other end of the line, at the time of the murder. The murderer was never identified.

★ ★ ★

During those heady early months together, spring turned into summer. Ben and Louise went on long hand-holding walks along the Regent's canal, and up on the Heath. They watched obscure *mittel-Europaeische* movies *(mit Untertitlen)* at the Everyman, and sat uncomfortably on a blanket, picnicking to the sounds of an orchestra on the other side of a lake at an open-air concert at Kenwood House. They sat perched high up on the seats of the Regent's Park Open Air amphitheatre and enjoyed a performance of 'Porgy and Bess', Louise surprised by how many of Gershwin's songs she knew, and another time when they had seen a Shakespeare production Ben persisted in calling 'Omelette'. Ben took Louise to a gig by the former guitarist in The Slits, the seminal all girl punk band, who was performing at 'The Roundhouse', the former engine shed in Chalk Farm, and to 'Underworld', a music venue underneath the 'World's End' pub. A pub they knew, once upon a time, had been 'The Mother Red Cap', a famous 'Half way house', where water had been drawn from a pump in the street, and nearby houses backed on to fields where haymaking and cricket were the primary pastimes during the day, but by night 'watchmen', with twinkling oil lamps on sticks, mounted patrols to protect the local inhabitants from 'footpads' lurking behind the hedgerows under the cover of darkness.

* * *

Ben and Louise's summer strolls also took them south, to Mornington Crescent, named after the Earl of Mornington, brother of the Duke of Wellington (Ben, putting on a Michael Caine accent: 'Not a lot of people know that.'), the one-time elegant terrace of Victorian houses hidden behind the former Carreras 'Black Cat' cigarette factory. The building that dominated

83

the crescent since its controversial construction in 1928 as 'The most modern, hygienic cigarette factory in the world'. An art deco masterpiece with Egyptian motifs, the vogue back then, the recent discovery of Tutankhamun's tomb having captured the popular imagination. Where, according to a local history book, two black cat effigies, stylised versions of the goddess *Bastet*, the protector, flanked the entrance (a black cat being a branding device for Carreras' Egyptian tobacco-filled 'Craven A' cigarettes). Where the façade of the building was painted with colourful details of papyrus plants and cat's whiskers and, at the rear, the factory chimney masqueraded as an obelisk.

The blighted views from the front of the terraced houses, combined with the rail tracks running hard behind, inevitably led to a reduction in social status and the houses gradually converted to multiple occupancy flats popular with Irish immigrants, mostly single males, navvies, who had migrated to north London for work on the canal and railway. It had become a squalid backwater, and the perfect muse for Sickert who, according to a blue plaque, had lived at no. 6.

- XI -

Louise pregnant

The previous week: nothing. Not a drop. She was never late. Not this late. Had she lost too much weight? She weighed herself on Vicky's scales, only to discover that she was actually slightly heavier than before. Give it another week she thought, at the same time thinking she better not put on any more weight. If there was any irony in her situation, it was completely lost at this time on the usually pin-sharp Louise.

The week passed. It had been just after 11pm, a weekday night. Still nothing. There was school tomorrow. Louise knew she should sleep, but she couldn't. She lay there, on her back, staring at the ceiling. Superficially random yet intrinsically linked thoughts chasing each other round her head on a relentless loop.

The hiss of tyres on the wet tarmac outside would occasionally intrude. As would the sound of voices approaching, ever louder and rowdier in the street below. Kicking out time at the pub thought Louise. Young, white, working class men drunkenly making their way home, swearing, unconcerned that their voices were audible to those, like Louise, who were tucked up for the night behind the curtains and shutters of their terraced bedrooms. A flagrant disregard of the pub's notice informing them that, *'This is a residential area. Customers are respectfully requested to leave the premises quietly out of respect for the neighbours.'* Why use the word 'respect' only twice wondered Louise, on the one occasion when, slightly tipsy, she exited the rather seedy pub on the corner? Why not squeeze in another one? Or two? Or more? How about this, *'This is a respectable residential area. Customers are respectfully requested to leave the premises quietly out of respect for the neighbours. 'Spect'.* Hic!

Across the landing, Louise could see that Vicky's light was still on. She made her decision. She climbed out of bed wearing Ben's boxers, his faded orange '24 Hour Service' t-shirt hanging loosely off one shoulder. She liked to sleep in Ben's clothes: it meant she could feel close to him, breathe in his smell. It was a way of sleeping with him every night without waking up feeling sore, or still tired.

Louise didn't knock, when had she ever needed to knock? She pushed at the door and slouched in disconsolately, the first time she had been in Vicky's bedroom for a while. Vicky was sitting on top of the covers in her pyjamas, the ones with the giant rose pattern, looking all pink and clean after a bubble bath with the drops of that ylang-ylang essential oil she liked, the pungent, musky smell still permeating the entire flat. Vicky's head was resting against the headboard, her open MacBook warm in her lap. She had earphones in and was watching something intently as the door swung inwards and Louise appeared with big pleading eyes swimming in their sockets. Vicky started, and in one quick movement half-closed the lid of her laptop and yanked out the earphones. Louise had made her jump. She thought Louise was fast asleep. Her light had been out. Louise, in her self-absorbed state, hadn't registered anything.

Vicky had to move her leg out of the way swiftly as Louise slumped down onto the bed without heed, hunched over, both hands now up to her face. She began to sob silently. Vicky watched Louise's thin shoulders moving up and down, one exposed, revealing a grouping of tiny moles, like a celestial constellation. Vicky forgot all about herself and leaned forward, wanting nothing more now but to comfort her best friend. Had something happened between her and Ben? Louise dabbed away at her eyes with a soggy tissue, now uselessly balled up in her fist. After a short while she composed herself, sat upright and straightened her shoulders. Vicky waited. Louise, her face puffy and her eyes red.

"I think I might be pregnant."

It was the first time Louise had said the 'P' word out loud and, having finally uttered it, it became a fact. She knew it to be true.

"How long?"

"Almost four weeks."

"Have you done the test?"

"I've been too scared."

"Do you want to?"

"Yes."

Louise had replied in a small voice, so uncharacteristic thought Vicky. All the questions were left there, hanging in the air. Vicky put an arm around Louise's shoulder.

"It's too late now, nothing will be open. We'll get one tomorrow."

Vicky spoke soothingly, stroking Louise's bedraggled hair.

"I've got one."

"What?"

"I've already got one."

"Oh… Shall we go and do it?"

Louise blinked and nodded almost imperceptibly.

* * *

She recognised she had been a bit unfair towards Vicky over the past few months, and there was no denying that Vicky felt Louise had somehow betrayed her by going off with Ben. They had been having such a great time, and then Louise had spoiled it. She had grown close to Ben in such a short time. They were spending so much time together and Vicky had been excluded. Three or four times a week now Louise would stay overnight at Ben's. She no longer even bothered to let Vicky know in advance.

At first Louise would call and they would chat for a while, inconsequential stuff. Later she would send a text to say she wouldn't be coming home. Then even texts were evidently deemed unnecessary. Fact: Louise no longer cared about her and how she might be feeling. Vicky felt lonely in the flat on her own. She found herself waiting up, or lying in bed unable to sleep, like a fretful parent, waiting for the reassuring sound of Louise's heels clipping up the stairs, inserting her key in the lock, perhaps unsteadily, one or two attempts – it didn't matter, she was home. Vicky had begun to feel resentful, she felt Ben had robbed her, snatched Louise away from right under her nose.

Oh, she liked Ben well enough. Everybody liked Ben. You couldn't help but like Ben. He was good-looking, funny, charming. A good guy. She could see exactly what Louise saw in him. She knew he was good for her, that he was unlikely to hurt her, but somehow this made it worse. There was nothing she could say or do other than pretend to be pleased for Louise. Which she was, obviously, in a way, but it was still unfair and Vicky found herself wanting to cry out, 'What about *me*?'

In response, retaliation almost, Vicky started going out more often after work, mostly with colleagues from her magazine, deliberately not telling Louise in advance. But it wasn't as much fun as going out with Louise. On more than one occasion Vicky had been out for the evening and, judgement impaired, she would find herself waking up with the consequences lying next to her and an increased self-loathing. With Louise effectively gone, Vicky realised that what she really wanted was her own Ben, but he was not proving easy to find. 'How many more *fucking* frogs?' she thought.

★ ★ ★

With dragging feet, Louise walked back to her own bedroom; Vicky followed and stood at the doorway. From her handbag on the floor Louise retrieved a white paper bag, carefully folded over and sealed at the top, a green cross on the side. Sitting on the bed, Louise tore open the bag and the receipt fell out onto the floor. She took out the box and turned it around, scanning the instructions but was having problems, she couldn't focus properly. The words were not making sense. They were swimming in front of her eyes. All she wanted to know was what meant 'yes', and what meant 'no'. Why didn't it just tell you that? Surely that was the whole purpose of the bloody thing! Vicky stepped into the room and took the box from Louise, taking charge, she knew how the test worked. Vicky broke the seal with her nail and removed one of the plastic white sticks. She looked at Louise and beckoned. Louise got up, followed Vicky to the bathroom.

★ ★ ★

Louise handed the wet stick back to Vicky and roughly grabbed a bunch of tissue from the roll. She stood, pulled up Ben's boxer shorts and flushed the toilet. They walked in file back to Vicky's bedroom and climbed under the duvet where, with straining eyes, they stared at the little window, waiting for a coloured line to appear. Under other circumstances, it was just like old times. When they would share a bed and talk before lights out.

There it was. Vicky broke the silence.

"We'll do another one in the morning. Just to make sure." More silence. "What will you do?"

"I don't know."

"Will you tell Ben?"

"Yes. Of course. I love him."

"What do think he'll say?"

"I don't know."

"Do you want to keep it?"

"Yes."

"What about your job? How will you manage? And Ben?"

"I don't know."

They lapsed back into silence once again, Louise burrowed into Vicky's shoulder. She really was her best friend she thought before briefly dozing off, relieved to know finally, and be able to unburden herself to Vicky. Vicky who had always been there for her. Vicky, who needed her too, but was now selflessly looking after her instead. Again. Whatever happened with Ben, Louise knew that Vicky would still be there for her. But Louise no longer wanted Vicky, she wanted Ben. She knew she would willingly sacrifice Vicky if it meant she could be with Ben. Did that make her a bad person? The fact that she could abandon the one person in the world she knew she could depend on. Who was there for her right now when she needed her. The one person who knew her as well as she knew herself, probably better. The one who knew things about her that Ben would never, ever know.

★ ★ ★

Louise was so fearful. He said he loved her, but what would he say now? Would he blame her? Would he run away? What might he ask her to do? Would it all be over? They had been having so much fun and she had gone and ruined it. She felt guilty. She felt as though it was all her fault. What did she really want? No, she was sure she knew the answer to that... didn't she? How would she cope? This had not been on the agenda at all. Talk about putting the cart before the horse. They had told each other so much stuff, had talked about so many things, but they had never talked about babies. She steeled herself and studied Ben's face intensely as she told him the news, trying to gauge his real reaction, his true feelings.

Ben's initial disbelief, followed by the inevitable, 'How?' and 'When?' gave way to tumultuous emotions, a mixture of thrill, more disbelief, a bit of shock, and a trace of fear, but, overwhelmingly, a desperate attempt to try to get his head around what this meant. Ben was stupefied. What *does* this mean? What were the implications? But then he had grinned at her, a big grin. Perhaps a slightly odd reaction, but Ben realised he was actually pleased with himself: he'd got Louise pregnant. And he wanted the baby. Ben didn't bother to ask what Louise wanted.

"This is big Louise, this is huge. It's bigger than huge, it's... mammoth!"

Louise's anxious face lit up in the most wonderful way. She tossed her head back and then from side to side, dark brown hair swinging in front of her child-like face. She let out a curious, almost animal sound, a cross between a yelp and a shriek. Ben didn't even hear it. Louise's expression changed again. She felt so much love for him at that moment; her eyes shone, filled up and overflowed. Ben held her face in both his hands. They looked intently into each other's faces seeking unspoken words from lips, and then into each other's eyes, flicking from right to left and left to right, as though one eye might possibly reveal more than the other. The same thoughts tumbling through their heads, not necessarily in the same order.

Once the incredulity faded, Ben had absolutely no doubt, no hesitation. It was still sinking in, he still didn't quite know what it all *meant* – they would work that out – but he knew he wanted this baby, a baby with Louise. He loved her; he wanted to be part of this. He wanted to share this thing. Their thing.

Ben was even more certain now. He had known

it for a while. He wanted to marry Louise. Commit. True, they were both still young, at the beginning of their careers, and who knew where their careers would take them, but you can't put a date on these things, you can't schedule a timetable for love. Sometimes you just have to go with the flow. Anyway, they were going to have a baby. He would ask Louise to marry him. Not just yet, but soon, very soon. He must prepare for this properly. You only have one chance to get this right he thought. It would become family folklore, their reply to friends' questions at dinner parties. What they would one day tell their child.

It was a while later before it dawned that a baby meant a likely corollary for his other love, the two-seater sports car.

- XII -

Ben proposes… a short holiday

"But doesn't it always rain in the Lake District?"

"But this is August! Anyway, if we don't go now, who knows when we'll get the chance again."

An unspoken reference to the baby, currently not much bigger than one and a half centimetres, tiny, suspended in an amniotic sac, but set to grow rapidly over the next few weeks and then, within a few short months change both their lives forever. Already Louise felt bigger. Her underwear and jeans tighter, or was that just her imagination?

Acknowledging that the weather could be changeable, Ben, put on a thick northern accent.

"Besides, you know what they say? No rain… no lake."

They had both arrived early, but separately at the Caribbean restaurant, straight from work, and were sat at their usual table. Ben in a navy blue suit (he'd met some clients that day), tie less, Louise in dark trousers – although it was the school holidays Louise was on a course in a central London hotel – *'How to be an Outstanding Middle Manager in an Independent School'* – and had come to associate 'work' automatically with trousers. After all, you couldn't be too careful sitting on chairs designed for five year olds, especially with the leering, odious deputy head prowling around. She was also wearing a green – her favourite colour – v-necked blouse, her hair tied back in a stubby ponytail. Ben thought Louise looked fantastic, and expectant, in all senses.

* * *

Louise was questioning Ben's choice of the Lake District for a mini-break to celebrate the pregnancy. Couldn't they go somewhere hot? But Ben had his own ideas and was now trying to sell them to Louise. He may have hated camping, but he loved fell walking – as long as he had somewhere warm and comfortable to return to at the end of the day. He had been to the Lake District several times, the first had been on a school trip, staying in a youth hostel, where he had met a pretty Belgian girl called Carina. Ben had lost his virginity to Carina and retained very fond memories of her and, consequently, the Lake District. He told Louise all about this small corner of England, sandwiched between the famous industrial cities of the northwest and the Scottish border. A magical place of glacial lakes, forested valleys, remote wildernesses, epic views, tumbling waterfalls, mysterious stone circles and, literally, thousands of miles of incredible, physics-defying dry stone walls. Although he was reminded of her, Ben thought it best not to mention Carina.

Ben had a thing about dry stone walls. He knew all about them. They had captured his imagination: the labour, the man-hours that had gone into building these, now yellow, grey, green moss and lichen covered boundaries with their stone stiles and kissing gates. Walls delineating what, exactly? Many seeming to serve no purpose at all, almost as though they were some kind of ancient job creation scheme, or the result of some early community service, a penance imposed by village elders, perhaps redress for misdeeds with another man's sheep.

Ben was explaining to Louise how the walls were constructed without any binding mortar (hence 'dry'), and that the reason this worked was because the weight on the outside leant inward to the core of the wall, each stone carefully selected to create a near flush contact to prevent slipping or wobbling. The most common construction practice had been to cut a narrow trench and lay down a base of stones. The wall was then built up in progressive layers, each narrowing slightly towards a centre which was filled with smaller stones until, at about two feet above the ground, a layer of 'through' stones would be laid across the entire width, to tie it together, and then it would continue upwards, to about four or five feet before, finally, being topped with a row of vertical stones.

He's finished thought Louise, but no, there was more. Ben, deliberately winding her up, maintaining a straight face, going on to tell her that these amazing constructions were not merely features of agricultural interest they were, he said, in a sense, living history. A legacy of the movement towards enclosure of common farming and grazing land as society moved away from feudalism. In fact, most of the dry stone walls we see today…

"Enough already!" cried Louise, trying to cover Ben's mouth with her hand.

"Okay, okay."

Ben laughed and pushed Louise's hand away.

"Then let me tell you about graphite. Graphite was discovered in the Lake District and led to a key development in the history of writing, so I know you'll find *this* interesting."

And he did tell her. Ben told Louise all about the 16th century discovery of a huge deposit of graphite near Keswick and how, initially, it had been used to mark sheep, but its limitations were soon exposed (when it rained, presumably), but then someone had the bright idea of casing it in wood and inventing, da-dah… the pencil! The world's first pencil factory was established in Keswick and demand for this new writing tool soared. The graphite ran out a long time ago said Ben, but the Cumberland Pencil Company ('Perhaps you've heard of it?') was still going strong.

"Bet you didn't know that many writers, including people like *your* Nabokov and Steinbeck, had considered the CPC's 'Blackwing 602' to be the best pencil, ev-err."

Louise allowed him go on. She knew what he was doing and gave him one of her trademark mock-pitying looks as Ben said that the pencil museum in Keswick attracted pencil lovers from all over the world. It was the 10th most visited tourist attraction in the Lakes. It was, he said, now he thought about it, probably wise if they booked tickets in advance. Louise agreed.

"It would be a terrible disappointment if we got there and couldn't get in."

* * *

Louise sensed that Ben was up to something. He was being unusually evasive on the detail of their trip to the Lakes, secretive even. In an effort to elicit some detail, Louise had offered to help him in the planning.

"There's really no need,' he said, "Besides, I want it to be a surprise, and it's not difficult. It's not rocket salad." Ben, as his wont, deliberately subverting an otherwise hackneyed saying.

He wouldn't even tell her where they would be staying. Louise didn't really mind, she liked surprises, and Ben was clearly enjoying himself. He seemed so happy. They were both happy.

* * *

Louise wondered if, up in the Lake District, Ben would

ask her to marry him. Vicky was convinced. She'd said it's just the sort of thing he would do, Louise chose to ignore the note of resentment in Vicky's voice.

If she had been asked before all *this*, Louise would probably have scoffed at the idea, it not really fitting with how she viewed herself. Even now, they needn't get married straight away she thought, or not even before the baby was born (she wanted to be a *bit* rock 'n' roll), but it would be a tangible sign of his commitment to her, and the baby, wouldn't it? Louise tried to push these thoughts aside. She didn't wish to dwell on the matter. She wanted to avoid at all costs any sense of disappointment when they got there; didn't want to spoil their first trip away together. Instead she told herself to just focus on enjoying being together. Being happy. Ben was so enthusiastic, it was clear he loved it up there, in the Lakes, and his enthusiasm was contagious. She wanted to go. There would be long walks and romantic dinners. They would fall into bed together. Lie in each other's arms, tired after a day out in the country air. She would breathe in his scent and they would make love, slowly at first, then the passion and force would take over. She loved giving herself up to him. He made her feel this way. No-one else had ever made her feel quite like this. There was no doubt in her mind, Ben was the One.

- XIII -

New chapter

Ben was annoyed. He'd forgotten the cable to connect
his iPod to the Mercedes' car stereo. He had planned to
set it on shuffle and play 'name that tune' with Louise,
all the way to the Lake District, confident of beating her
hands down. Now he couldn't.

There was always the radio of course, for in-
car entertainment, but they had discovered a shared
antipathy towards the radio. They spoke of mindless
DJs (the very name, *Disc! Jockey!*); the fake *bonhomie*
and irrepressible high spirits; grammatically-incorrect
banter; adverts; annoying jingles *('Jingles?')*; traffic and
weather reports... 'Phone-ins'!!? OMG, who were these
people? Why would anyone wish to allow disembodied
strangers' voices into their personal space? Unfettered
'access all areas' admittance to the inside of your head?
Telling you things you had no need or desire to know;
subjected to music you didn't want to listen to, hoping
against hope that the song that came next would at least

be tolerable, or if not that one, then the one after it.

It turned out that it didn't matter, not having any music in the car. Ben and Louise were more than content with each other's company: they exchanged stories, jokes and anecdotes. They entertained one another, they didn't need anyone or anything else, the whole journey underpinned, as it was, by anticipation. The miles and hours passed quickly, both deliberately avoiding any discussion of a future beyond the the next few days. Neither wishing to break the spell.

★ ★ ★

An old trick question.

"How many lakes do you think there are in the Lake District?"

Louise hazarded a guess.

"Twelve?"

"One."

Louise sat back in her seat and looked at him, arms folded, saying nothing, waiting for him to explain, knowing he would.

"One."

"One?"

"Yes. One. Bassenthwaite. Bassenthwaite Lake."

A pause.

"Go on."

"All the others are either meres, or waters."

Louise contemplated this for a moment.

"Er, *hullo?* Lake Windermere?"

"Exactly. It's Winder*mere*. Not *Lake* Windermere."

Ben, shook his head theatrically, conveying his disappointment.

* * *

With their future now inextricably intertwined (one way or another), in the car Ben and Louise spoke about the contrast between their relationship and the one they witnessed between their parents, both now and whilst growing up. Times were obviously different, and only two people ever knew what really went on in a marriage, nevertheless they agreed that they would never end up like their parents. Neither Ben nor Louise had suffered the pain, the inestimable consequences of coming from broken homes. Instead both sets of parents were long-married couples who, over the years, had developed a remarkable facility whereby they not only didn't need to speak to one another, they no longer really even saw one another. They communicated on a whole other level, looking through or past one another, managing somehow to navigate potentially hazardous marital waters without capsizing, running aground or colliding, like those thousands of tiny silver fish that, on some instinctive command, change speed and direction as one, or migratory birds gathering in sky, anticipating sunnier climes ahead. Couples who existed in a sort of connubial détente arrived at in the shadow of otherwise mutually assured destruction.

Ben and Louise's parents were throwbacks, the end of the line. Remnants of a raised-in-the-suburbs generation that still clung to a desire for post-war respectability in the face of a media-driven post-baby-boomer world. A need to keep up appearances for friends, family, colleagues. Making the best of things. Keeping calm and carry on using diversionary self-denying coping behaviours. They had 'settled'. They just got on with it. All mutual resentment buried in a shallow grave. The petty grievances, annoying habits and tiresome mannerisms. Personal traits that were once deemed cute, endearing even, that had become the embodiment of a dissatisfaction that, as the years went by, had become increasingly both mental and physical, resulting in the onset of mute blindness. Or so it seemed.

Occasionally they might wonder if it could have been just a little bit greener, on the other side, or, Heaven forbid… Emerald! What if they *had* acted spontaneously that time? Those times? Back then. What if they *had* responded differently to that impulse, that transitory but nevertheless all-consuming desire? That knowing, flirty comment, that moment, that opportunity. A nagging feeling prompted by a sudden memory, a daydream or a sexual fantasy, but a feeling nevertheless just as soon pushed down again. Suppressed.

★ ★ ★

They didn't talk further about their parents, but they did discuss religion during the car journey, still one of

Louise's pet peeves, and something which had turned her into a Richard Dawkins disciple, almost a militant atheist. The latest Islamist terrorist atrocity, still all over the news, had prompted her to wonder out loud if the jihadist ever stopped to think.

"Doesn't he ever question what he's being told?' she asked. "Is his life really that shit? Need it be? 'What if I've got this all wrong?' he might ask, 'There is no Hell. No Heaven,' and what exactly would either be like anyway, waking up, on a day to day basis?"

"Maybe I shouldn't cut off this guy's head, or detonate this vest after all? These people seem okay. Going about their business, with their kids. They've done me no harm. Some of them are probably muslim. What if there are no virgins waiting for me in Paradise? What if it's just a ruse? And wouldn't it be better to have just a couple of girls, white girls with a bit of experience? Wouldn't that be better? More satisfying? A threesome, isn't that every man's fantasy?" she asked, looking over at Ben who just shrugged his shoulders as if so say, 'I don't know, don't ask me!'

Louise continued. "And what reward does a female suicide bomber get? Does she get back together with her martyred husband? What about the seventy-two other women he's supposed to fuck. Women who, according to the 15th century writings of Ibn Majah, are 'Perpetual virgins with appetising vaginas'. Where does that leave her in the pecking order? Maybe it doesn't matter because, apparently, 'The penis of the Elected never softens. The erection is eternal.' Ibn Majah again. But what about love, family… babies?" Louise paused, her thoughts now ranging wider, encompassing other world religions.

"What if there is no reincarnation into another body? Or, going forward, past performance being no guarantee of a higher form of life."

Ben beamed. He felt a warm glow. He knew they were made for each other.

★ ★ ★

The evening before Ben and Louise set off for the Lake District, Louise had been in the flat, packing. Vicky was not home and Louise suspected this was deliberate. The flat had seemed eerily empty, as though ghosts were flitting around, the air disturbed, invisible bats hiding in dark corners, always just beyond view, no matter how quickly or unexpectedly Louise turned her head.

Louise found herself thinking back to that last day of term. Everyone else, teachers and children alike long since departed to their other lives, their real lives, but Louise, ever conscientious, had stayed behind to mark a raggedy pile of green and blue A5 exercise books. The school rooms were empty, a silence had descended like a fire blanket, but then, if you listened closely, you could still hear muffled high-pitched echoes of childish excitement seemingly coming out of the walls. It was still ages until her baby was due, but Louise wondered if she would ever return.

★ ★ ★

Louise set to packing, busying herself, selecting clothes to put into a large canvas holdall before reflecting that she didn't know what she should pack beyond the new stuff: the walking boots and one-size-larger jeans. Ben had been wonderful though, ever since she had broken the news about being pregnant, just ten days earlier, but she was finding the secrecy surrounding their trip slightly irksome now that it came to packing. 'What's a girl supposed to do?'

The holdall was nearly full. Louise looked again in the depleted wardrobe, at the forlorn hangers and plastic dry cleaner wrapping before pulling out another summer dress, stuffing it into the holdall, and then a green cashmere cardigan from the chest of drawers. A quick look around the bathroom to make sure she hadn't forgotten anything and then, with both arms and a knee, she manoeuvred the holdall off the bed and struggled along the hall towards the front door. She felt a pang as she turned the double lock. She wished Vicky had been there to say goodbye. To give her a hug, to wish her good luck.

* * *

One of the modules Louise had studied on her Eng. Lit. degree course was the 19th century Romantic Movement. A movement that had swept Europe and been a major influence in all areas of the arts. In the restaurant, when Ben finally wooed her with the idea of the trip to the Lake District, Louise said she wouldn't

mind going to Grasmere ('If your plans will allow!').
William Wordsworth was buried there she said, and
Dove Cottage, where he and Thomas de Quincey had
lived, was nearby. Both had been leading lights of the
Romantic Movement in England and Louise was keen
to visit the area which had inspired such wonderful
poetry.

Ben had been more than happy to incorporate
Louise's wish. He was pleased she was demonstrating
an active interest in the trip he was planning, planning
meticulously, in his head. This was good he thought,
this augurs well. Louise wasn't indulging him, she
would appreciate, she would understand, they would
share the joy.

Ben had factored Grasmere into his plans: they
would go there first. Leafing the pages of a water-
damaged guidebook, Ben identified a walk nearby,
one with a steady, not too onerous climb for Louise,
one that promised 'good views over the surrounding
countryside'. With a quiet satisfaction Ben reckoned
they could get up there in time for lunch in a favourably-
reviewed restaurant, do the walk and then visit the dead
guy's grave/house.

Ben calculated that if everything went to plan, they
would arrive at their final destination at the perfect
time of day for maximum impact. For the surprise that
would be waiting for Louise at the boathouse.

- XIV -

Road trip

It was bright and sunny when they'd set off early that morning. The night before Ben had been irrepressible, he'd cooked Louise his signature pasta dish, penne with walnuts and chevre blanc, telling her he'd gotten the recipe from an Italian friend, Al, Al Dente (Louise, giggling: 'Oh, puh-leeze!'). And today he remained energized by the prospect ahead. He wanted to get going. Louise, on the other hand, was content to stay in bed a bit longer, wanting to cuddle.

"Louise, c'mon, get up, the early bird catches the ball!"

This failed to do the trick. Ben shook her gently.

"Louise, time for *le petit dejeuner, il et huit-heures-bix.*" A rising oxytone on the final syllable.

This, at least, elicited a groan from under the covers, Louise recognising that Ben had begun to make fun of her *'occasionel'* French-isms.

★ ★ ★

It had been too chilly to put the roof down, but Ben had, nevertheless. It was in the plan, his vision, how he had foreseen things, and he was determined that nothing would change it. Pulling on the red button in the centre console he released the catches in the top of the windscreen frame. The roof lifted up and over their heads before disappearing completely into its housing behind the seats, entombed in a matter of seconds with a Teutonic clunk. The procedure still delighted Ben, though he did concede to Louise that the morning air was still a little 'fresh'. But no matter.

To counteract the freshness, Ben switched on the heated seats and then caused a blast of initially cold but increasingly warmer air to hit them: a two-pronged assault from dashboard and footwell. They began to warm up. Ben had thought this through.

The Finchley Road was unusually subdued and they joined the North Circular earlier than expected then, just as Wembley stadium's wire basket handle reflected a laser of sunlight directly into their eyes, they turned right, Ben accelerating up the ramp and onto the M1 where they followed signs to 'the North', as though the North was a precise location, a strange and different land. Which of course it is.

* * *

The journey proved uneventful but was enlivened, slightly, just before Luton, when they spotted the incongruous sight of two fire engines, lights flashing, racing along, flat out in the slow lane. Ben, along with everyone, else cruised past them at a stately 80mph. They joked that the flames would probably be out by the time the fire engines got there, and queried why they were called 'fire engines' - surely they should be 'water engines' or, better, 'water bowsers', wouldn't that be more accurate? At the approach to Birmingham, Ben took the M6 toll road. He could not take the chance of being held up by congestion around Britain's second city, not with the timetable fixed firmly in his head.

At around the half-way point of their journey, Ben sought to know more about this Wordsworth fellow Louise was so keen on. Although aware, obviously, that the Lakeland poets were world famous, Ben did not necessarily comprehend the veneration they were accorded. Unlike say local girl made good, Beatrix Potter, Ben telling Louise that, as a child, his favourite bedtime story was about Peter Rabbit's run-ins with Mr McGregor in the latter's vegetable patch. Furthermore, Ben was not ashamed to admit that a Peter Rabbit soft toy, blue jacket, no trousers, had been his constant companion for perhaps longer than otherwise considered usual, even for a young boy.

Louise, Ben discovered, was more than happy to expound on Wordsworth, and other poets, and on poetry in general, and at some length.

Wordsworth, she said, was arguably Britain's finest poet. He had been very influential amongst the Romantics ever since the publication of the so-called 'Lyrical Ballads' he had co-written with Coleridge in

1798. These had been revolutionary at the time she said: experiments in the use of the language and conversation of ordinary people, writing about rustic, everyday subjects. Many of Wordsworth's contemporaries, de Quincey in particular, had been in awe of him. Though to be fair, she admitted, Wordsworth did have his detractors too, not least Shelley and Byron, both of whom had ridiculed him.

Ben learnt that Wordsworth's most famous poem, one about some daffodils, had been inspired during a walk with his sister Dorothy in Gowbarrow Park on Ullswater. ('Hah!' Thought Ben. 'She has no idea that's where we're staying.') Dorothy had recorded the walk in her journal as, *'The happiest combination of beauty and grandeur which any of the lakes affords.'* Louise said that Wordsworth's daffodil poem was consistently voted the British public's second most favourite, second only to Kipling's *'If'* in the Great British public's consciousness – a poem, according to Louise, so saccharine it should carry a 'Type 2 diabetes warning'. Louise further opined that this was doubtless because these were the only two poems people ever remembered from school. Ben reluctant to display his ignorance was not absolutely certain which poem Louise was referring to.

"Can you just refresh my memory, about the daffodil one…?"

"I don't believe it! You must remember. From school?" she teased.

"Yes. No, of course. Come on, just tell me…"

"I wander'd lonely as a cloud? That one?"

"Oh yeah, God yeah, I know that one."

"Go on then."

"What?"

Ben looked at her quizzically.

"Obviously I don't know it *all*. Not off by heart!"

Louise, delighted to have a chance to show off to the father of her future child, began to recite.

'I wander'd lonely as a cloud
That floats on high o'er vales and hills,
When all at once I saw a crowd,
A host of golden daffodils,
Beside the lake, beneath the trees
Fluttering and dancing in the breeze.

Continuous as the stars that shine
And twinkle on the milky way,
They stretch'd in never-ending line
Along the margin of a bay:
Ten thousand saw I at a glance
Tossing their heads in sprightly dance.

The waves beside them danced, but they
Out-did the sparkling waves in glee:
A poet could not but be gay
In such a jocund company!
I gazed – and gazed – but little thought
What wealth the show to me had brought.

For oft, when on my couch I lie
In vacant or in pensive mood,
They flash upon that inward eye
Which is the bliss of solitude;
And then my heart with pleasure fills
And dances with the daffodils.'

Ben was impressed; and it did make a sort of sense, but for some reason he was unable to tell her either of these things. He was unable to demonstrate the pride he felt in her, or even acknowledge the erudition Louise felt she warranted. Instead, Ben found himself unable to control a primordial male reaction: a completely irrational need to gain the upper hand, to regain 'face'. Instead of telling her any of these things, Ben maintained that he still didn't really get poetry, and then he tried to goad her. He didn't mean this maliciously, but it would prove to be a grave mistake.

Ben said that, frankly, he had a problem with a cloud, 'Wandering in a lonely manner'. Didn't wandering imply legs? *'Floating'* maybe, he offered, before adding that he was also unsure about the idea of a cloud, 'Feeling *lonesome'* or, given its purely gaseous make-up, having feelings at all.

"Anyway, isn't poetry all rather… effeminate?"

It wasn't working, Louise was irritated but refusing to respond, to rise to his bait. Over the relatively short time they had been together, she had come to learn Ben's little tricks all too well. She wasn't going to fall for this one. Louise stared ahead resolutely, straight out of the windscreen, apparently focussed on the car in front. She pretended she wasn't listening. That she hadn't heard him. There was a new silence in the car that Ben tried to ignore, before pushing on regardless, compounding his mistake.

"Why do new lines start in the middle of a sentence? How do you know where to pause? And the words, some of the words are ridiculously obscure, words that no one ever used in real life. Come on Louise, '*jocund*'? Life is too short, who can be bothered?"

Still nothing. Then almost to himself, "Often they don't even rhyme."

Finally he was getting a reaction. Ben enjoyed watching Louise become animated, passionate about something, to see her in teacher mode, that deep twin vertical furrow on her brow. He was proud of her; he saw in her both an inner and outer beauty. He admired her intelligence, the way she challenged him and the fact that she could make him see things anew. The way she could hold her own in any company. He also felt unbelievably lucky that this girl should love him, actually love *him*. He was sure of this. The things she said, the kind and thoughtful gestures. Her smile, and the way she laughed at his little jokes and sayings. The look he would see in her eyes. The way she affectionately touched him or would unexpectedly fling her arms around his neck and kiss him, stretching up on tiptoes. The way she held onto his arm when they were out walking, or simply sitting there on the sofa. The way she clung to him in bed, needing him there, unwilling to let him go, even in a deep sleep.

They made a fantastic team he thought. Ben had never been happier in his life.

★ ★ ★

Louise, however, was having very different thoughts and was no longer able to contain herself. She could not let him get away with this. She finally took the bait, swallowed it whole. 'Right', she thought. 'He's asked for this. *Philistine!'*

Louise sat forward in her seat, Ben noticed the seatbelt delineating and defining her breasts, but failed to read the body language. Louise launched into a vigorous defence of poetry. She began to lecture him, adopting a patronising tone as though speaking to a particularly dense pupil. She told him that reading a poem was not like reading a book, or a magazine. Its aim was not to impart knowledge or provide information. It was a totally different experience: shorter, concentrated, intense and emotional. A poem demanded full attention; you needed to take time, sit down in a quiet place. You can't read poetry standing up. You can't skim it or rush it seeking to extract the essential message. You have to read a poem several times to understand it, to appreciate it properly, to savour it.

"Look at the poets from the First World War. They are not just telling you that war is bad and sad. Everyone knows that, or that the reader should really try to take this on board and learn from it. They are more poignant… More poetic."

116

Louise regretted it as soon as she said it. She was furious with herself: she'd just told Ben that poems were poetic. It was now Ben's time to look away, to concentrate on the road ahead. He knew he shouldn't, but he found himself grinning. Louise soon rallied.

"The poet's aim is to work within established rhyme and meter. Do you even know what that is? To use words in surprising ways, unexpected ways. To use literary devices, imagery, irony, figurative language, metaphors, similes. Things like alliteration and onomatopoeia, plays on language and letters. Ideas such as, 'I wander'd lonely as a cloud,' should not necessarily be taken literally."

Louise said all this in a withering tone. As for being effeminate, Louise reminded Ben that these poets were the 'rock and roll' rebels of their time, forcing the public to look at life in a completely different way. De Quincey and Coleridge were drug addicts. De Quincey had actually written a book called, 'Confessions of an Opium Eater'! Coleridge regularly took laudanum, but was also a pioneer of rock climbing. Lord Byron was famously described by Lady Caroline Lamb as, 'Mad, bad, and dangerous to know,' but it didn't stop her pursuing this 'bad boy' relentlessly, scandalously even. There had been persistent rumours that Wordsworth had an incestuous relationship with Dorothy, and that he had a daughter from an affair with a French woman. A daughter he didn't see for ten years because of the Napoleonic Wars.

"You wouldn't describe the alcoholic, womanising,

Dylan Thomas as effeminate, would you? He used to lived in Camden too you know, Delancey Street."

Louise was relentless, the bit really between her teeth now. She told Ben that, should he ever decide he wished to have a go at reading a poem, he should avoid the common mistake of trying to maintain a rhythm at the expense of concentrating on the actual poem. It was important to understand a poem first, she said, before he could read it properly, Ben should go through it two or three times in his head first, ignore the "formatting", Louise choosing the word deliberately, miming inverted commas with bunny-ear fingers for Ben's IT consultant brain. Just because a line on a page might end she said, it didn't necessarily mean the end of the sentence, normal rules of grammar still applied: you pause when you reach punctuation. That's what it does. Punctuate!

★ ★ ★

This was a new Louise and Ben wasn't sure he liked it. He hadn't seen her quite like this. He was embarrassed. He had no idea what had come over her. Louise continued. There was more.

"If you don't have the patience to tackle a long poem, no worries!"

If he liked, she could help him start with a really short one, an easy one. If he still found it difficult, he should let her know, she would help him distinguish between what he did and didn't understand. Twisting the knife, Louise told Ben that he shouldn't be afraid to look up any words he didn't know, or was a little bit unsure about, that's what dictionaries were for. You could learn new words, expand your vocabulary. Become more articulate.

Louise stopped abruptly, as though she could finally hear herself. Why was she haranguing him like this? She was being deliberately insulting. Poor Ben, look at his face! She had hurt him. Louise slumped back in her seat, a hand to her mouth.

"Oh my God! Just listen to me. Ben, I'm so sorry. I don't know what's wrong with me. I'm turning into a real bitch. Please forgive me." Then quietly to herself, "I must be a terrible teacher."

Something had just happened there but neither understood what it was. Something had just changed between them. Ben was completely abashed, stung. He'd been joking! Why was she treating him so? He decided to try and gloss over the incident as quickly as possible. Get things back to normal. Forget what had just happened. It *hadn't* happened. A ridiculous overreaction. His fault as much as hers. An aberration. She hadn't meant to attack him personally like that. It was surely just excitement, the baby, the uncertainty; she must be overwhelmed by conflicting emotions.

But Ben didn't know what to say, how to respond in the thick silence that filled the car like cotton wool. He just sat there as Louise began desperately to try to deflect, to de-personalise her attack on him. She apologised again, voicing a general complaint that poetry was overlooked these days. That people were missing out on something that could be so rewarding, something that could bring unexpected pleasure. She despaired, she said, of today's children. Kids seeking to validate their entire existence through social media. No one had the time to unlock poetry, she said, let alone lose themselves in the pages of a good book.

Over to Ben. It was now his turn. He tried to demonstrate to Louise he was not completely ignorant. He told her that he really liked the poem by that lanky miserablist bloke, the guy with the pebble glasses, Larkin, that was it. The guy who had written about how your mum and dad 'Fuck you up', but Ben quickly realised that he couldn't recall anything of the poem beyond this infamous line. He would try again, desperately wanting to lighten the atmosphere, get things back to normal, to how they had been just a few minutes ago, but this was stretching out into an eternity. Then he had it. It came to him.

"Have you heard of a guy called Morecambe?"

"What? …Who?"

"Morecambe."

"Morecambe?"

"See those cows grazing on yonder hillock? This time tomorrow, that grass will be millock."

Louise couldn't believe it.

* * *

Ben began to tell Louise a story from his school days. He must have been about eleven. A story involving the

120

only other poem he could remember, although it wasn't really a poem, not like the ones the other children had rehearsed, but lines he would never forget nevertheless, the one he had chosen for an English lesson. A poem he had memorised the night before. Homework. A poem he would have to recite in front of the whole class the next day. Ben relived the whole experience out loud for Louise.

It had been his turn, he said. The teacher, Miss Baines, a tall thin bespectacled spinster in her mid-fifties, invited him up to the front. Ben had pushed back his chair, scraping the floor noisily, and sauntered with an exaggerated gait up to stand in front of the blackboard (this was before whiteboards he explained to Louise, as an aside who, glad for any reprieve, encouraged him to get on with it). Ben had faced his classmates, all eyes were on him. Ben told Louise that his heart had been pounding so much, he could hear it and believed that everyone else must surely be hearing it too. Did he really dare do this? Could he get away with it? But he was up there now, and she was there, Clare, directly in front of him. Everyone was waiting, impatient. It was too late he realised, he had no choice, there was no going back. He didn't *have* anything else.

Ben said he had cleared his throat and taken a deep breath. Then, with a nervous but unwavering gaze, he spoke directly to her. To Clare Browning, the girl sitting there at her desk in the front row. Clare with the thick blonde hair, chopped crudely and held from her face with a plastic grip. The quietly studious girl in regulation knee-high navy socks and, Ben knew, navy knickers. The girl whom all the boys had a crush on. The girl who had never, not once, acknowledged any of Ben's adoring puppy dog glances.

Ben had been a bright pupil, sometimes a bit too clever for his own good, and sometimes he would play the class clown, a bid to remain popular, or at least not be bullied by some of his less clever, potentially violent classmates.

When he had finished, and it hadn't taken very long, the entire class was left open-mouthed, gaping. There had been astonished shrieks, some involuntary squeals even. As one, all eyes had swivelled away from Ben. They were now trained and fully focussed on Miss Baines, all apart from Clare's. Clare kept her head down, red-faced in unwarranted shame. If she had previously felt indifferent towards Ben, she now felt something akin to hatred, but everyone else, all the other children were holding their breath, suspended in a horrified fascination at the scene unfolding in front of them. The children did not yet have the vocabulary to do justice, to adequately describe what they were feeling when Ben finished. Who could have guessed that Miss Baines' English lessons could be so…compelling? English was not an 'option' subject for GCSE, but if it had been, the entire class, minus one perhaps, would have signed up straight away.

Ben had done it. He'd said it. He felt an intoxicating mixture of elation and trepidation. A tidal wave of adrenaline flushed through his body as he walked back to his desk, light-headed, feet barely touching the ground. Any pretence to acting cool now way beyond him. He sat and waited, eyes down, studying his grey-scuffed school shoes, the unravelled ends of his shoelaces. He'd done it alright, and now he could not look in Miss Baines' direction. You could have heard the proverbial pin drop. Everyone was waiting. What would Miss Baines say? What would she do? He couldn't say that! He couldn't get away with this, surely?

After all the other kids, the ones before Ben, Miss Baines had led a short class discussion on their poems, but not this time, not after Ben. Instead, Miss Baines had squinted, pursed her lips and requested, in a flat voice betraying no emotion, that Ben remain behind after class. Then, looking down at her clipboard, called out the name of the next pupil on the list.

Louise, equilibrium restored, felt awful. How could she have been so horrid to Ben? She would definitely make it up to him later but, right at this moment, she found herself drawn once again into another one of his stories. She knew he was dragging it out, making her wait, but she still loved it. He had stopped speaking, pretending to concentrate on his driving. She knew he was waiting for her to ask, and he knew she would. Louise owed him his little bit of fun and so shook her head, an exaggerated movement causing her hair to swing to and fro. A mannerism Louise had appropriated from one of the little girls in her classroom, and which Ben had told her he always found sexy. Louise let out an exaggeratedly resigned sigh.

"Go on then. What was it?"

After prolonging the moment for as long as he felt he could get away with, Ben began to recite the poem or, more accurately, verse. The one where he had deliberately substituted the words at the end from 'are' to 'have', exactly as he had done all those years before when he had spoken directly to pretty little Clare, in the presence of his teacher, and in front of the whole English class.

Ben intoned,

'The Owl and the Pussy-Cat went to sea
In a beautiful pea-green boat.
They took some honey, and plenty of money
Wrapped up in a five-pound note.
The Owl looked up to the stars above,
And sang to a small guitar,
'O lovely Pussy! O Pussy, my love,
What a beautiful pussy you have,
You have!
What a beautiful pussy you have!'

Once again Louise turned towards him in her seat, but this time she was jabbing him in the ribs with a forefinger, a doomed attempt to get him to stop; he was making fun of her, responding to Wordsworth with Morecambe and bloody Wise, and then nonsense verse by Lear. Ben, with both hands clasping the steering wheel, was ill-equipped to defend himself from the assault on his left flank, yet he managed somehow, in between involuntary yelps, to finish and, looking directly at Louise, stressing the penultimate word, he repeated the line.

"Oh what a beautiful pussy you have."

★ ★ ★

They exited the toll road, rejoining the M6 proper and, sure enough, just around Manchester the clouds began to gather and the temperature dropped. Ben pulled into a service station to fill the Mercedes' tank once again – it really did empty at an alarming rate. Ben was enjoying the car, and he loved the smell of petrol, but that 5.0 litre engine really did drink the stuff.

He went in to pay. Another £100. Ben made a mental note that he must be getting perilously close to maxing out his credit cards, he would need to be careful. Only a few weeks ago he'd had thousands in the bank, but there had been the car, the ridiculous cost of the boathouse for just a few days (though it was high season, and it did look fantastic on the website), and finally the four-diamonds-in-a-line engagement ring ('That's a whole bunch of carats' he'd remarked to the giggling sales assistant in the tight, button-straining blouse in the New Bond Street store). Ben felt for the box deep in his trouser pocket as he headed back towards the car where Louise was waiting. He smiled at her through the windscreen, hiding his concern. She returned it, giving him that beautiful one that lit up her whole face. They were back to normal.

With the roof now raised, they continued north. Not too much further to go, but still time enough to tell Louise the joke about the guy with the massive orange head. The joke he had told so successfully not so long ago in The Mockingbird (and probably, he thought, what had made Gnat want to fuck him). Time enough to make Louise laugh, make sure she loved him again.

- XV -

The guy with the massive orange head

"Did you hear about the guy with the massive orange head?"

Here comes another one she thought, before looking over at Ben, rolling her eyes and doing the head shaking thing again. She did love him.

"Go on then."

"A guy with a massive orange head walks into a bar. His head so massive that he has to hold it up with both hands. The guy with the massive orange head goes and sits on a stool in the corner. Everyone in the bar stops and stares at the guy with the massive orange head, holding up his massive orange head with both hands.

The barman saunters over cautiously to the guy with the massive orange head and asks the guy with the massive orange head what he would like to drink. The guy with the massive orange head says he would like to have a Coca Cola, please, with a straw. The barman asks the guy with the massive orange head whether he would like ice and lemon with that. The guy with the massive orange head, using both hands, nods, 'Yes,' he would like ice and lemon with that.

The barman walks back up the bar to get the guy with the massive orange head his drink. Using both hands, the guy with the massive orange head turns his massive orange head to watch the barman select a glass from the shelf and put in ice and lemon. The barman then snaps open a bottle of Coca Cola and slowly pours the carbonated liquid into the glass and over the ice. Finally, with a flourish, he adds a straw. The barman then heads back towards the guy with the massive orange head sitting on the bar stool in the corner, holding up his massive orange head with both hands.

The barman places the Coca Cola with ice, lemon, and a straw in front of the guy with the massive orange head. The guy with the massive orange head says thank you to the barman who remains standing there, watching as the guy with the massive orange head lowers his massive orange head, supported by both hands, to sip the Coca Cola with ice and lemon through the straw.

The barman asks the guy with the massive orange head, 'How's it going?' the guy with the massive orange head replies that it's going fine, 'But I expect you would like to know why I have this massive orange head.' The barman admits that he would like to know why the guy with massive orange head has a massive orange head. The barman ventures that perhaps the guy with the massive orange head had been bitten by an insect, or had suffered an allergic reaction. The guy with the massive orange head, supported by both hands, shook his massive orange head, 'No, but it's a very long story.'

The bar is not busy, so the barman says to the guy with the massive orange head, 'Go on then', and the guy with the massive orange head begins the story of how he got the massive orange head that is so massive he needs to support it with both hands. The guy with the massive orange head tells the barman how, one day, he was walking along a fine golden sandy beach with his dog, Rover, and how Rover was running into the sea, coming out, shaking himself, and then running back into the sea again, 'You know how silly dogs can be,' said the guy with the massive orange head. The barman nodded and the guy with the massive orange head continued with his story.

The guy with the massive orange head told the barman how Rover suddenly began digging frantically in the golden sand. Rover was digging and digging, said the guy with the massive orange head. Sand was flying everywhere. Digging and digging. Why was Rover acting this way the guy with the massive orange head had asked himself, but it wasn't long before the guy with the massive orange head said that he too got down and started digging too, with his bare hands. Of course, back then his hands were free because he did not yet have a massive orange head which he needed to support with both hands. The barman was intrigued.

He urged the guy with the massive orange head to continue." Ben was enjoying himself, aware that Louise had begun fidgeting in her seat, playing with her hair, letting out little sighs, wishing he would get on with it. It never failed! Ben continued.

"Finally, said the guy with the massive orange head, he and Rover unearthed an old-fashioned lamp, an oil lamp that had been buried deep in the golden sand. The guy with the massive orange head thought it must have lain there for many years because the metal had oxidised. The guy with the massive orange head went on to describe to the barman how he had begun rubbing the lamp, polishing it on his pullover and so on, and how, all of a sudden, there had been a loud bang accompanied by a puff of smoke. The guy with the massive orange head said he had been startled, but this soon gave way to alarm because, as the smoke cleared, it revealed… a genie.

The guy with the massive orange head described the genie's appearance to the barman. How he had a black moustache that curlicued at the ends; how he had worn a green turban, how the giant golden earring in his ear had dazzled the guy with the massive orange head whenever it caught the sun, how the genie's massive chest had glistened with an oily sheen and, said the guy with the massive orange head, how when he folded his arms the genie displayed big, powerful biceps, triceps, forceps." Here Ben had improvised, just to see if Louise was still paying attention. "The genie towered over the guy with the massive orange head. He must have been at least ten feet tall, swaying out of the spout of the ancient oil lamp, a dramatic vision against an azure sky above the golden sandy beach.

The guy with the massive orange head said he was relieved when the genie looked down benignly upon him and, in a deep commanding voice, said to the guy with the massive orange head, 'You have freed me from a thousand years of captivity in this lamp buried deep in the golden sand of this beach. I will grant you three wishes.'

The guy with the massive orange head explained to the barman that this had never happened to him before and he'd been a little bit stumped. The barman had shrugged his shoulders and nodded to convey his complete understanding.

After a short while, the guy with the massive orange head said to the genie that he would like to be incredibly wealthy. No sooner as he uttered the words, 'incredibly wealthy', then gold coins rained down onto the beach, all around the guy with the massive orange head. The genie said, 'You are now incredibly wealthy,' and asked the guy with the massive orange head what he would like for his second wish. The guy with the massive orange head had put his head in his hands to help him think (not because he needed to support a massive orange head he said, reminding the barman once again that he was yet to possess a massive orange head). The guy with the massive orange head explained to the genie that this sort of thing didn't happen to him every day and he would need a little time. The genie encouraged the guy with the massive orange head to take his time, pointing out

131

that after a thousand years trapped in the lamp buried below the golden sandy beach, he was in no immediate hurry. There was nowhere he needed to be.

Then the guy with the massive orange head made his decision. He said that for his second wish he would like to marry the most beautiful woman in the world. The genie smiled knowingly, 'They're all the same,' he thought as he parted the waves in front of the guy with the massive orange head and a Venus-like creature walked up the beach towards him. She was the most beautiful woman the guy with the massive orange head had ever seen and, with just a few words, the genie pronounced them man and wife. The guy with the massive orange head was now not only incredibly wealthy, but he was also married to the most beautiful woman in the world.

'Now for your third and final wish,' said the genie to the guy with the massive orange head. The guy with the massive orange head furrowed his brow. This was trickier than he expected. I have everything I could possibly want now thought the guy with the massive orange head. But then the eyes of the guy with the massive orange head widened and, in a tentative, voice, hardly daring to ask, he finally spoke up, 'Would it be possible,' he asked the genie, 'would it be at all possible to have a massive orange head?"

Ben couldn't help it. He began to laugh. Louise said it was the stupidest joke she had ever heard. She also said she loved him even more as Ben considered that this really did work with the 'lay-dees'.

- XVI -

Arrival in the Lakes

After just over four hours, there it was, the first
motorway sign: 'The Lakes'. Ben and Louise adjusted
themselves in their seats, sat more upright, became
more alert. Ben began to slow down, and flicked up
the indicator stalk with his index finger, preparing to
change lanes, preparing for the exit.

★ ★ ★

Unbelievable thought Ben, as large spots of rain began
to appear on the windscreen. He resisted switching
on the single window wiper for as long as he could.
Neither he nor Louise said anything. The rain fell
more heavily and Ben no longer had a choice. He stole
a glance at Louise. She was smirking.

"Go on, say it."

"Say what?" Louise wide-eyed, feigning incom-
prehension.

"Go on, say it," repeated Ben, "the rain."

"I don't know what you mean. I knew all along it would rain. I expected it."

Louise laughed and punched him playfully on the arm. Ben didn't want to mention that his arm was feeling sore after gripping the steering wheel all this way.

Louise said she really didn't care about the rain.

"I just want to be with you, sweetheart, whatever the weather, come rain or shine."

* * *

"Look! There's one."

Ben had spotted his first dry stone wall and was pointing it out to Louise. He spoke of how it almost felt like coming home, and how he was so happy to be sharing this moment with her.

The rain eased off as they approached the outskirts of Windermere, the town itself actually a mile distant from the north eastern shore of the lake of the same name. Ben found himself swerving into the oncoming lane to avoid large puddles of rainwater flooding the sides of the road. Then they were in Windermere, with its Victorian villas and hotels, stern-faced patriarchs fashioned out of granite and slate. They sped on past the railway station that had brought the line up from Kendal in 1847, directly into the heart of the Lake District. The railway that had heralded the arrival of mass tourism to the region.

Wordsworth, regardless of having published *'A Guide through the District of the Lakes'* in 1810, a volume he described at the time as being for the, 'Minds of persons of taste', and which he regularly updated, deplored this incursion of the great unwashed and had even written to *The Times*. Wordsworth chose to ignore the fact that this new tourism industry was to become a lifeline for the inhabitants as it gradually replaced the traditional industries of farming, mining and quarrying which, even then, were in decline.

★ ★ ★

Out the other side of Windermere and on to Ambleside. Ben and Louise caught their first glimpse of the dull grey lake as they sped downhill, water spraying from the wheel arches, on past the sports centre and through the ancient Roman centre of Waterhead and Borran's Park, where ducks and swans now ruled the grassy banks once inhabited by an occupation force of leather-skirted Centurions.

Ambleside, with its own imposing stock of grey-green hued buildings, but here they were interspersed with low-rise terraces of B & Bs with their 'Vacancies/ No vacancies' flip-signs hanging in net-curtained windows.

★ ★ ★

Ben was stuck in Ambleside's one-way system, in the wrong lane. Several cars refused to let him manoeuvre into the right one, choosing to believe the driver of the flashy sports car with the pretty young girl was arrogantly trying to queue jump (they didn't know Ben). It was only after the cars backed up behind him started beeping that someone relented and let him into the long line waiting for the traffic lights. Lights which refused to be hurried, but neither this, nor anything else, could spoil the good humour which had returned within the compact cabin of Ben's car.

"I spy, with my little eye, something beginning with G."

Louise ventured some guesses.

"Grass?"

"Nope."

"Glass?"

"Nope."

"Gear...knob?" She said, testing Ben. Seeing if he would do one of his sniggering 'Beavis and Butthead' impressions (he didn't, not this time).

"Nope."

"Gridlock?"

"Er... Nope. Give up?"

"Yes."

"Gnome... I spy with..."

"Don't wanna play this game!" Louise exclaimed, interrupting him, pulling a face and doing that head shake thing once more.

They edged forward slowly before coming to yet another halt. It was Louise who kicked-off their usual game, importing it from London: imagining the lives of the locals, the people behind the curtains of the houses all bunched up together, lining both sides of the street right up to the lights. It was sparked by a B & B advertising that it offered heating. Ben and Louise chipping in alternately, trying to out do each other with comments about housecoated landladies, straight-jacket beds with coarse blankets, counterpanes. Overstuffed rooms. Fully fitted swirly carpets. Bathrooms with electric showers and a u-shaped rug around the toilet bowel. Carpet everywhere. Even on the toilet seat. And avocado hand-basins where, however hard you tried to wash them away, trails of soap and spat out toothpaste would always reappear.

They went on. Airless 'lounges' with 'real coal effect' heaters. Armchairs with machine-washable Dralon covers. Antimacassars! Laminated Microsoft Word instructions for guests affixed to doors and walls with blue-tack or worse, drawing pins. Printed in a jaunty, rainbow-coloured font following the landlady's helpful young nephew's experimentation with computer and printer settings, an attempt to soften the commands.

Neither Ben nor Louise meant any unkindness. They weren't judging (who were they to judge?). They told themselves it was a game of imagination based on observation, and they delighted in bouncing off each other. An affirmation that they remained on the same wavelength, were as one.

* * *

Ambleside had proved reluctant to let Ben and Louise escape its clutches, but they finally managed to break free from its gravitational pull and emerge onto the Rydal Road where they pressed further north. The rain had stopped and the sun was really trying as Ben, enjoying himself immensely, swept along the undulating road, catching further flashed glimpses of water through the trees.

Heading away from the water now, at a junction marked by some whitewashed cottages, they turned left onto an old packhorse road where, nestling at the base of a backdrop of unbroken fells, lay the village of Grasmere.

Grasmere

Every tree and every lamp post along the road into the village bore a poster advertising the forthcoming Grasmere Sports. An annual competition of running, jumping, and sheep dog trials. Trials conducted in a secret language: singular commands of 'bye', 'cast', 'steady', all conveyed with a movement of the hand, a flat, crescent-shaped whistle, or a shout, or a combination of all three. The games, traditionally held on the third Thursday after the first Monday in August, originated in ancient times and had managed to retain their popularity into the present, attracting thousands of visitors each year.

Ben parked up amongst the metal mass of cars, minibuses and coaches in the ugly car park on the edge of the village. They clambered out, unfolding themselves, stretching arms and legs. After the rain, the air was so fresh you could almost taste it. The light had changed too: everything in sharp focus and stark contrast.

It was early afternoon and Ben and Louise were hungry; they'd had nothing to eat since a round of toast with an orange and ginger fruit spread in Ben's kitchen that morning. Already in their walking boots, they retrieved jumpers, a guidebook and a map from the boot and set off on foot into the village.

The pavement was crowded with a broken procession of day-trippers and walkers in brightly coloured cagoules. There were a lot of dogs on leads, all shapes and sizes, four-legged versions of their owners. At one point Ben and Louise were forced into the road by a young group of excited, camera-toting Japanese, most likely English Literature students suggested Louise, hogging the narrow path with the youthful disregard of others.

Ben said he was reminded of a story ('When aren't you?' thought Louise) and began telling it as they continued their way into the village. He had been with some friends he said, driving a hire car along a typical narrow lane bounded on both sides by tall hedgerows, somewhere between Lakeside and Cartmel, somewhere well off the beaten track, wide enough for only one car at a time but with designated 'passing places' carved out at 150-200 yard intervals. Of course two vehicles would often meet head on, and a sort of Mexican standoff would ensue but, being English, one party would soon back up, very unlike in the 19th century incident in Central America Ben said, which gave rise to the expression. Where two powerful families, their horse-drawn carriages heading in opposite directions, entered a narrow street and met halfway. They couldn't pass but both refused to give ground, each insisting that the other back up his carriage. An impasse. Both parties stayed firm for several days, their servants supplying them with food and water until, finally, the authorities had no choice but to intervene, forcing both parties to retreat. Ben added ruefully that, unfortunately, history didn't record what happened next.

In Ben's story however, in his incident, the other car, a silver Ford as it happened, immediately went into reverse, the engine protesting loudly as it pulled back fifty yards at an alarming speed. As Ben edged forward to pass, door mirrors almost touching, he acknowledged the other driver with the customary nod and wave, and was about to accelerate away when the rear window of the Ford slid down and the head of a young Japanese woman appeared, followed by an arm which began waving in front of his windscreen, forcing him to brake, and then, an anxious voice, 'Soh wee, soh wee, we lost! Where Lake Distric?'

Completely non-plussed, Ben said he had gesticulated mutely to indicate that they were in it. It was all around them. When Ben recovered his voice he told them that this was the Lake District to which she had replied, 'Ah so! Tank oo vay mutch.'

The Japanese lady, head bobbing, appeared relieved before her expression turned into a newly-confused frown, her arm remained outstretched, almost, but not quite touching the glass in front of Ben's face, unwilling to let him drive off, yet culturally acutely conflicted, 'Ho kay, ho kay… But where lake?'

Ben said he remained stationary as the silver Ford finally inched past and drove off, leaving Ben staring at a vandalised sign where the car had been shortly before. A sign which now read, 'Pissing place'. God knows what the Japanese had thought.

★ ★ ★

Ben and Louise trudged over the humpbacked bridge into the village, the shallow water below fast flowing yet crystal clear, the smooth-worn stones on the riverbed clearly visible. They continued past the ascetic St Oswald's Church on their right, agreeing to visit Wordsworth's last resting place later because, right now, they really needed something to eat.

They followed a hand-painted sign pointing down a small lane. Tiny cottages on one side, and a high dry stone wall on the other with green fields beyond, Ben steered Louise to the favourably-reviewed restaurant for lunch. They would need to fortify themselves he said, before tackling the 1200ft peak of Helm Crag.

The dining room was no bigger than someone's front room, the tables pushed close together, creating an intimate setting, possibly too intimate. Fortunately there were two or three empty ones, and Ben and Louise were directed over to one for two shoved up against a far wall. The waiter was immediately upon them and began a run through of the day's esoteric specials, all of which went straight in one ear and out the other as Ben and Louise, engrossed in each other, virtually ignored him and his disappointment as they opted for Cumberland sausages and mash (Ben: 'When in Cumberland…').

Waiting for their food to arrive, Ben read aloud from his guidebook, telling Louise about Grasmere's 'coffin trail', how it dated from medieval times and was the name given to the path across White Moss Common from Rydal to Grasmere. The route along which coffin bearers had 'toiled to St Oswald's with their sorrowful burden', the book conjuring up an image of six men led by a priest, head bowed, clutching a prayer book, a line of straggling mourners following on behind: men in leather tunics and stockings, women in smocks, low-cut surcoats and bonnets, musicians too, producing suitably mournful music on lutes and flutes, a drum keeping everyone in step.

★ ★ ★

Un-be-liev-able thought Ben, once again. They were back out in the narrow lane when the skies opened and a steady rain began to fall. Holding hands, Ben and Louise ran back into the centre of the village, pausing to catch their breath under cover of a bus shelter and consider their next move. The rain turned out to be a short-lived shower, but it was clear that, even in August, they would be foolish to undertake their walk without proper wet weather protection. Ben, having convinced Louise it wouldn't be necessary, should really have known better.

On the other side of the road, just up from the bus shelter, they spied an outdoor clothing shop advertising an 'up to 50% discount'. They splashed their way through puddles over to the store and, fifteen minutes later emerged wearing 'his-n-hers' 100% guaranteed waterproof jackets with detachable fleece linings. One in pink, one in blue, investments in their future together, and a bargain at half the RRP.

★ ★ ★

Retracing their steps, they headed out the other side of the village on a steadily climbing road, the houses on either side gradually thinning out as the road narrowed. A hundred yards beyond the last house they turned right, up a track, following a public footpath sign and disturbing a grouse pecking away at its base. It ran away at their approach with its peculiar gait. Ben, not normally strong on birds, knew a grouse when he saw one, recognising it from the label of the malt version of the famous whisky he had recently begun developing a taste for.

Brushing against bracken weighed down with globules of water which, if you bent down and peered closely, contained upside down miniatures of their surroundings, Ben and Louise continued to climb through intermittent showers. After about half an hour they came across a lone walker holding aloft a black broken-winged umbrella, carefully picking his way down towards them. After the impersonality of London, one of the things Ben enjoyed out on the fells was the exchange of greetings whenever you came across another person. Ben volunteered a friendly 'Hello' to the stranger under the umbrella who revealed himself to be a young bespectacled Japanese male who smiled and bowed from the waist in acknowledgement. Ben and Louise stood aside to let him pass before exchanging glances and raised eyebrows as if to say, 'What is it with the Japanese obsession with our Lakes?'

They continued to climb, now over boulders, before emerging onto a slippery grass track. They passed hardy Herdwick sheep, spray-painted fleeces, smit marks, denoting ownership and/or origin, a doughty breed able to survive on the rugged open fells and said by Ben, though greeted disbelievingly by Louise, to eat their own wool if nothing else was available.

"See that black-eyed sheep over there? That's Wool.I.AM. And the little one next to it, that's L.A.M., the black one of the family... C'mon Louise, s'funny!" Ben had been working on his material during the climb.

* * *

The going became quite tough in places and they had to side-step sheep droppings littering their way. Occasionally they would stop to look back down over the path they had climbed, measuring their progress. The broken umbrella now a distant black dot bobbing below in a sea of green.

The low grey sky and gradually fading light of the afternoon was causing colours to bleed into each other, lending the view a melancholy appearance. Ben absolutely loved it. He realised anew that he was never happier than when out walking in the Lake District, out there in the elements. In fact, he was wondering if he had ever felt happier than he did right now: positively luxuriating in the sheer physicality of it all out there on the fells, sharing it with Louise, there, right beside him in her new pink jacket. Her wild dark hair plastered to her forehead, long damp strands hanging down in front of her eyes. The woman who, although she didn't know it yet (or did she, with that intuition thing they had going on?), he was going to ask to marry him that very evening. The woman who, in a few months time was going to give birth to a little Ben, or a little Louise. How fantastic was *that*? Ben had a preference for a girl but had made a solemn vow to himself not to betray this to Louise, not wanting her to think he would be disappointed if it should turn out to be a boy, which would be fine too.

* * *

During one of their increasingly frequent pauses, Louise, tiring but otherwise serenely happy, surveyed the majesty around them.

"It's beautiful," she said, "brooding... Bronte-esque!"

"It's positively Wagnerish," responded Ben assuredly, managing to finally go one better, for the first time trumping Louise in the cultural reference stakes.

Ben went further, he told Louise that at moments like these a *'Ride of the Valkyries'* soundtrack would sometimes start up in his head, like a wind-up gramophone. He would have visions. He would see a horn-helmeted, sword-wielding Wotan singing to Bruennhilde, played by a hefty Heidi from Hannover, or racy Renata from the Rhineland, anyway, someone with big powerful lungs barely contained by the plunging neckline of a frilly white blouse. Someone built for comfort, not speed, in an ill-fitting, possibly slightly askew plaited and pig-tailed blonde wig. Someone looking and sounding for all the world like Miss Piggy. Louise laughed out loud. No one else had ever made her feel the way Ben did. How was it possible? Right now, she loved him even more.

* * *

They continued upwards and after several false peaks and a treacherous traverse of the ridge, reached the summit of Helm Crag. What happened next, as though heralding their arrival, was something Ben, for all his meticulous planning, could not have scripted, not in a million years: a rend in the hitherto solid bank of cloud in the distance. The sun's rays an irrestible force flooding through the fissure and across the fells, illuminating everything in their path, bathing Ben and Louise in yellow light, forcing them to shield their eyes as the wave washed over them and on into the next valley. A watery rainbow appeared in the far distance.

Ben felt... What did he feel? He felt blessed. It doesn't get any better than this he thought, and with the upraised palm of his right hand and the forefinger of his left, he turned to face Louise and said, "Give me a high six!"

★ ★ ★

Viewed from the top of Helm Crag, Grasmere, the Langdale Pikes beyond, and the suspended mirror of Easedale Tarn off to the right, were all in the glare of the sun's spotlight. A spotlight that also illuminated further rain clouds on the horizon.

"Every cloud has a silver lining Louise, but, equally, every silver lining has a cloud..."

★ ★ ★

Looking directly up into the sky from their already lofty vantage point, Ben and Louise experienced simultaneous vertiginous sensations as they watched what they believed to be the magnificent frayed wingspan of an eagle circling high above them. They didn't know there were no longer any eagles in England, that the last one had died a lonely death a few years go.

It couldn't therefore have been an eagle, it must have been a different member of the raptor genus, a buzzard perhaps, or maybe a vulture, vultures having been spotted recently in the UK.

* * *

Ben and Louise studied the map, seeking a different route back down to Grasmere, but it was obvious there was no way they could descend the other side of the crag as they took it in turn to peer over the ridge, holding onto each other for safety. Not only was there no discernable path, it was almost a sheer drop. The cars crawling along the A591 hundreds of feet underneath them, giants' playthings, inconsequential squashable bugs.

Ben and Louise had no option but to descend along the same route they had climbed. However, once back down, instead of returning along the same road village, the map showed that if they crossed into the meadow visible below and entered the woods beyond, they could follow the path beside Easedale beck to the packhorse bridge which would lead them into the village once more.

* * *

They began their descent carefully, conscious that the wet stones and boulders underfoot were far more treacherous going down than they were on the way up.

When Louise's boot slid away from her, Ben managed to grab and steady her, more than ever aware of the baby, his baby, growing inside her, entrusted to her for safe keeping.

It was almost an hour later when they reached the bottom of the crag. Safely back in the narrow lane and, with aching knee joints from the descent, they stopped awhile to watch a couple of blue tits playing kiss chase in and out of some bushes, Ben unable to stop himself: 'They make a nice pair' he said, before supporting Louise over a stone stile into the meadow and continued to hold her hand as they picked out a trail through waterlogged grass to the path that followed the twists and turns of the stream as it pursued the course of least resistance.

At a further stile they paused to look behind them. Back along the valley, the Easedale Tarn no longer visible from this lower elevation, but they could see the silent white waterfall cascading off the fell in the distance, water which, by the time it reached them had turned from white to black in the fast flowing beck in spate, lapping over the meadow path and around their feet before disappearing into the woods ahead.

* * *

Ben and Louise had no idea that Easedale was named after a tragic couple who died in a sudden blizzard, leaving behind six young orphans. A reminder, if they had known, that being out on the fells demanded as

150

much respect as being out at sea. It was scarily easy to lose your bearings when a sudden mist descended; or to slip down an unseen crevice. Or even hypothermia, as the temperature when you set out that morning plummets in the afternoon and you are soaked to the skin by ice cold rain. Out there Mother nature could suddenly turn on you and, with total indifference, reduce you to the fundamental organism you were. Render you with your social status and parochial concerns completely redundant in one stroke. Leaving you feeling naked, vulnerable and frightened. Leaving you with just a primeval desire to survive. At any cost.

* * *

Ben and Louise were back in the village, tired, but sharing a sense of achievement. A tacit acknowledgement that they had passed some sort of essential examination of their relationship, with flying colours.

After refreshments in a cafe, they headed over to St. Oswald's, the church named after an early King of Northumbria who, for some reason, had been promoted to Saint. Neither Ben nor Louise were inclined to enter the unprepossessing building where de Quincey had married a local farmer's daughter (a match looked down upon by Wordsworth and which led to a breach in their friendship).

Instead, they followed a sign directing them along the graveyard path to the rear of the church. Here, shaded by yew trees, they found the simple graves of

Wordsworth, his sister Dorothy, wife Mary, and three of his daughters, all lying side by side, for eternity. A time-ravaged Celtic cross just behind them bore the name Hartley Coleridge, the poet's son.

Louise's pilgrimage completed, they left the graveyard, out the other side, to what was once the village schoolhouse where Wordsworth had taught and which, today, housed a gingerbread shop where a cake consisting of molasses and flavouring was made on the premises following a 'secret' recipe kept locked in a bank vault in Ambleside ('Yeah, right!' they thought). Louise went in and bought a small packet, an edible memento, but its tooth-shattering hardness meant that it would shortly be consigned to the bin.

With tired but happy limbs conscious of every walking-boot step, they tramped along the road to the car park where they folded themselves wearily back into the Mercedes to drive the short distance to Dove Cottage, the second of Louise's riders for this trip. Dove Cottage, a humble whitewashed dwelling where much of Wordsworth's prolific output had been written until his expanding family forced him to move elsewhere, and de Quincey took over the tenancy. Back in the day, Wordsworth and de Quincey had an inspirationally clear view over to the lake but, at some point, inexplicitly, newer houses had been permitted, had been built directly in front of Dove cottage.

* * *

Ben and Louise decided to forego the guided tour offered by an earnest young man, preferring to wander around on their own. They entered a dark kitchen with stone flags, wood panelling, a fireplace, and a window seat to make the most of what little natural light managed to penetrate the room. Everything had been perfectly preserved. It didn't take a huge leap of the imagination to picture the Wordsworths living there but, otherwise, it was rather disappointing and contained little of interest: they couldn't muster much enthusiasm for Wordsworth's ice skates. Even less for Dorothy's sewing box. The most exciting artefact was a small pair of balancing scales engraved with 'T. de Q' on which de Quincey allegedly mixed his opium ('With what?' they wondered). There was a cuckoo clock, brought back from a trip to Germany – no doubt an enchanting novelty on the hour, every hour, for Wordsworth's brood, not the naff souvenir it would be considered by today's more demanding, prematurely jaded kids. Ben and Louise wandered out into the garden – apparently Wordsworth had been a keen gardener – but again they were rather underwhelmed by what they saw there: basically, just a garden.

Next door, a former coach house had been converted into a museum containing original manuscripts, portraits, and Mary's wedding ring. It all seemed a bit desperate to Ben, but he was happy to do this for Louise, the necessary give and take, the compromises, that would be an inevitable part of their life together.

Louise, for her part, having insisted that they

undertake these visits, and having banged on about poets and poetry on the drive up, felt obliged to show a greater interest in the museum than she truly felt, as though her credibility was at stake. It wasn't long however before she gave up the pretence. She was actually far more interested in discovering what Ben had planned next. Whenever she had asked him for details, he had just smiled and said he wanted it to be a surprise. She didn't even know where they were staying that night. Her concern more to do with being prepared for whatever Ben had in store. Being able to respond in the right way. *Éventualités*. To look nice for him. She should have bought some new shoes, instead she had just bought the boots, and the jeans, a size larger than she had ever worn before.

- XVIII -

The Struggle

The weather continued to clear up. The sun came out again. On the roads, disparate patches of light grey tarmac, the Resistance, were uniting, joining together to repel the damp darker grey Occupation forces, forcing them into retreat. Turning the tide, as it were. It was looking likely that, barring heavenly reinforcements coming down on the side of the dark greys, the light greys would win today's battle in the eternal Precipitation Wars played out in the Lakes.

★ ★ ★

By now it was late afternoon. They were back in the Mercedes, and it was warm enough to lower the roof once again, provided they kept their new jackets on.

Ben was full of anticipation, excited about what lay ahead. Louise felt excitement too, but hers was tinged with an unaccountable trepidation. Ben turned to

155

Louise and told her how he had always wanted to do this. This. What they were about to do.

★ ★ ★

'This' was not something Louise could possibly have anticipated. 'This', it turned out, was crossing one of the few Lakeland passes that wound their way through the mountains and fells connecting otherwise isolated communities, and about how Ben had always dreamed of doing it in an open top sports car and, with a playful slap on Louise's thigh said, "With my gal by my side."

Ben couldn't wait yet, at the same time wanted to prolong the moment, extract maximum pleasure, every last drop.

Finally, before resolutely putting the car into 'D', Ben reflected that he had never felt such contentment as he did at this particular moment in space and time: he had this wonderful woman, yes, woman, sitting in the passenger seat of his car, carrying their baby. He had absolutely no misgivings about her answer when he would propose to her, at dusk, at the boathouse on the lake. The proposal he had planned so carefully in advance with the connivance of Bill, the caretaker, over many phone calls ('Hi Bill, it's Ben'), and his wife, Peggy.

Just before re-entering Ambleside Ben turned off left, onto a steeply climbing road, a twisty route aptly known locally as 'the Struggle', originally a drover's track along which livestock were driven to market, impassable in deep winter. Ben gunned the engine, just knowing it would make thrilling short shrift of the 20% incline which would climb 1300 feet over the next three and a half tortuous miles.

The effortless power of the engine allowed Ben to revel in the burbling exhaust note as he pressed the accelerator, exiting sharp corners before having to brake hard to allow an oncoming vehicle, usually an SUV, all power bulges and flared arches, as though on a diet of steroids, to pass in the opposite direction.

They reached the top where, on a precipitous incline, they gave way. Peering over the bonnet they could see the whitewashed Kirkstone Pass Inn, the third highest pub in England, over five hundred years old and which, the bar staff will cheerfully tell you, is haunted. Ben indicated to turn left onto the pass, the automatic gearbox holding the car steady – no need for any awkward clutch balancing thought Ben as he continued to peer up and over to the right, waiting for a break in the traffic of cars and masochistic, lycra-clad and helmeted cyclists.

With the roof down, the temperature was noticeably lower up on the pass, where fells on all sides rose yet higher, but it was not long before they were speeding down towards Ullswater, a mis-shapened sliver of silver, just visible in the distance.

Ben told Louise that he had once stayed at the Kirkstone Pass Inn. It was on the same trip where he'd encountered the lost Japanese tourists, and how, in the late evening, under low wooden beams, a cadaverous barman with a funereal demeanour had kept him and his mates, gathered there around the dying fire, entertained with the tale of a local woman named Ruth Ray. It had been a winter's day said the barman, Ruth was on her way up from Patterdale, on a visit to her sick father, and taking her young child with her, but the weather turned for the worse. Snow began to fall. Ruth and the child failed to return that afternoon. Ruth's husband went searching for her, climbing along the same route Ruth would have taken. Night fell, it was viciously cold and the weather continued to deteriorate, so much so that soon the husband was in some trouble as well. He would have died up there said the barman, if he hadn't heard the barking of a sheep dog that guided him to a nearby farmhouse. In the morning, the husband set out again on the search for his missing wife and child, this time accompanied by the farmer. They eventually found them. Ruth was stone cold dead, but the child, wrapped in her shawl, had survived by some miracle. To this day, he said, the ghost of Ruth Ray haunts the Kirkstone Pass Inn...

"Good night lads."

"Have *you* seen it? The ghost?" Ben and his mates had asked, almost in unison. But the barman had theatrically turned off the lights and had suddenly disappeared, leaving Ben and his mates, the last guests, to reflect in the orange embers of the fire.

Turning to look at Louise at the end of the story, Ben saw she had tears in her eyes. He was mortified. Okay, the young mother had died tragically, he hadn't meant to upset her, it was just a story, probably not even true. There are no ghosts. Ben was baffled, he had no clue that the changing levels of oestrogen and progesterone during the first trimester of Louise's pregnancy would lead to such an intensification of emotions and unpredictable mood swings. Louise quickly recovered her composure however and wiped her eyes, assuring Ben she was okay. She apologised for, 'being stupid,' Ben took a hand off the steering wheel and squeezed her knee.

* * *

They swept through Patterdale, then Glenridding and continued out along the road that hugged the lakeshore. Even in the now fading light it remained, in Ben's view, one of the prettiest drives he knew. The road then climbed away from the lake and Ben eased off on the accelerator, looking out for the hotel on the right which would indicate a turning, a driveway that would lead back down to the water. Bill had warned that it was easy to miss, but Ben spotted it and stopped in the middle of the road, making sure it was clear before steering across the white line and pulling up at a metal gate with a hand-painted sign, 'The Boathouse'.

- XIX -

The boathouse

"We're staying in a boathouse?" cried Louise wide-eyed, excitedly, her hand clutching Ben's arm. "Oh wow," and then, "Could this *be* more romantic?" in a passable impression of Chandler from 'Friends'.

Ben grinned inanely as he drove slowly down a narrow puddled track, past an honour guard of fir trees, sentinels stood to attention on either side. 'Wait until she sees it' he thought, before emerging into open fields. One side empty land belonging to the hotel up on the road, its former owners having built the boathouse back in Victorian times, the other side fenced in fields full of sheep.

White-tailed rabbits disappeared into the hedgerow at the unexpected intrusion of the car. The huge gunmetal expanse of Ullswater lay ahead of them, water and sky separated by the magnificent fells rising from the far shore. Edging on downwards, the track disappeared into a clump of trees at the water's edge.

Then they saw it, a typical Lakeland stone building with a pitched slate roof. It looked tiny from this angle, now parked in the gravel driveway, but Ben knew from the Internet pictures that this was deceptive, and that the interior had Tardis-like properties.

* * *

They got out the car to explore. To the left was a wooded area, trees right down to the water's edge, their moss-covered skeletal roots exposed through the water's erosion of the soil. There was a pebble beach littered with driftwood. It all belonged to their boathouse. They skimmed stones and stared out over the lake together, drinking it all in. To the right was a patio area with chairs, a table and sun loungers, the patio bordered by a low flat-topped wall which led round to the front, to a narrow stone jetty protruding into the water, crudely concreted-in mooring rings set into the stone, and the jetty itself ending in a wooden landing stage which had either partly rotted away, or had been torn loose during a storm. In the near distance, a dozen or so uninhabited yachts, white-hulled with blue, red or green furled sails, anchored out in a natural bay and in stark contrast to the natural setting, all of them doing a sort of slo-mo synchronised mooring, a line dance, turning in unison whenever the wind changed slightly, or the wash from the last of the day's steamers ploughing along the opposite bank, a kilometre away, reached them. 'Aquatic caravans' remarked Ben dismissively. He really didn't like camping.

Steamers was a misnomer. The green and white boats with their red funnels were no longer steamers. Originally operational in the 1850s, they had delivered mail, workers and goods to and from the Greenside lead mine at Glenridding at one end of the lake to Pooley Bridge at the other. The two eldest, 'The Lady of the Lake' and 'Raven' had been converted to diesel in the 1930s, and when the mine finally closed down in the early sixties, were reborn as ferries for the increasing number of tourists to the region who were keen to get out on the water.

* * *

Ben and Louise watched contentedly as half a dozen mallards, in single file, paddled towards the shore where they waddled up into a field, their webbed feet seamlessly exchanging water for land as they entered a field where the sheep were constantlly grazing and baa-ing, ewes and lambs in a call and response. The mallards were settling down for the night, necks folded back, beaks nestling into feathers. Ben and Louise hugged each other. So far, this was living up to Ben's expectations, and Louise was being carried along by the sheer romance of it all.

Arm in arm, they turned away from the water and headed back to the rear of the boathouse, to the low wooden door leading into the wet dock. Ben recovered the keys that Bill had secreted earlier that afternoon and they descended the few stone steps. Ben unpadlocked the door and stood aside to let Louise go first, even Louise having to duck down to enter the doorway.

'JESUS CHRIST!' thought Ben, jumping out of his skin as Louise let out a nerve-shredding, bowel-emptying scream.

* * *

When she entered the wet dock, Louise's face had gone right through a giant cobweb. A shocked and disgusted 'Ughhooh' sound immediately giving way to the scream. Louise swiping away frantically at her face and shrinking into herself in dread of unseen arachnids.

Ben grabbed her and held on protectively, brushing away all traces of spider silk from her face and hair as fast as he could as Louise gradually recuperated, her heartbeat returning to something like normal. They continued into the boathouse, Ben now gingerly leading the way, Louise's arms clasped around his waist, still fearful, past two faded orange life jackets hanging listlessly from crooked nails hammered into stone, down onto a narrow gantry with a rickety handrail stretching almost the length of the wet dock. It was huge, room enough in there for several boats. The gloaming light, dissected by slatted gates framed by a stone arch at the far end, disclosed just one however, an eight-foot wooden rowing boat.

Their eyes were adjusting. They ventured further along the gantry. The boat was secured fore and aft in the shallow water by weights and pulleys affixed to the roof. A couple of inches of stagnant water sloshed around in the bottom. In peeling gold letters on the side, they could make out the boat's name, 'Angie'.

★ ★ ★

Ben considered it dark enough now to finally venture inside the converted accommodation above their heads, Ben hoping Bill, and Peggy, who had been chuffed to be involved, had followed his instructions to the letter, literally. This was it thought Ben as they both headed back along the gantry. Ben wanted it to be perfect. He didn't want anything to strike a wrong note. And it was perfect, almost, and although something would be struck, it wouldn't be the wrong note.

★ ★ ★

He'd had little time to plan, but with the caretaker's cheerful advice and practical assistance, Bill and Ben had been able to organise everything, Bill confirming to Ben that he had received the package and yes, it had been possible to run an extension cable outside. Bill assuring Ben more than once that he need not worry about anything. Everything would be fine. Bill and Peggy had wished Ben 'good luck'.

★ ★ ★

Ben selected an oversized key from the ring. It slipped easily into the lock and turned smoothly in a well-oiled mechanical movement. Ben pushed open one of the double oak doors and stepped back once again to allow Louise to enter first, which she did, but with more caution following the spidery ambush in the wet dock below them. She needn't have worried though. Not this time.

Just inside the door, on the mat, lay an ivory-coloured velum envelope, a Smythson of Bond Street notelet featuring a seahorse. Early on, when Ben discovered Louise had a thing about seahorses, before she got to know him better, he had queried whether they really existed ('Aren't they really, like, mermaids? Have you ever seen one?' Louise: 'No' she hadn't actually *seen* one, 'But they do exist. Damnit!')

Louise bent down. There was nothing written on the outside, presumably a welcoming note from the owners. But how did it get there? There was no letter box. A bit odd she thought. Why hadn't they put it on a table, or the kitchen counter? With the unopened envelope in one hand, Louise took in the scene. Wow! It looked fabulous, just like something in a magazine, or a brochure. With Ben close behind, they entered directly into a neat, well-equipped galley-style kitchen: combination microwave oven, Dualit toaster, Nespresso machine and a colourful selection of coffee capsules, a Sage juicer and a KitchenAid kettle. There was a bottle of wine, old-looking, a Cote-du-Rhone judging by the shape, a cream label with black and red script above and below a line drawing of a *chateau*. A roughly-hewn wicker basket full of foodies' goodies.

To the right of the kitchen was the bathroom, behind the space-saving sliding door was a walk-in shower with a rainfall shower rose; fluffy white bath towels; folded and bound his 'n' hers hooded bathrobes. One pink, one blue, just like their new waterproof jackets!

After Ben's prompting, Louise opened the envelope still clutched in her hand but forgotten about as she was taking in the interior of the boathouse. Louise extracted a thick card and, turning it over, saw a large '?' written in fountain-pen ink. What? She turned to Ben who performed a gallic shrug without fully meeting her gaze. He looked distracted. What's going on? Ben was focussed on something beyond her and was pressing his hand into the small of her back, gently pushing her deeper inside the boathouse. She stumbled slightly on one of a number of Persian rugs scattered on the stone flag flooring. What was going on? Oh God! Was this it?

Beyond a dining table set for two was a distressed brown leather sofa and a cream chaise-longue. A wood-burning stove was flanked by heavy oak cupboards, further on still were some dividing doors. Ben was gently manhandling Louise towards them. 'What's he doing?' she thought and then saw a second, identical, seahorse envelope, balanced on twin door handles. She plucked it up, opened it. The same blue ink. This time Ben's handwriting, unmistakeable, despite the capital letters. It read, 'Mary-Louise Adams…'. She looked up at him, but Ben was pulling aside the folding doors to reveal a bedroom. It was a bit gloomy, but Louise couldn't mistake the huge bed covered in cushions, a bouquet of red roses in the middle, a redness rendered redder by the crisp white linen. Ben had agonised over the flowers and the wine. Weren't roses corny? A cliché? Peggy assured him this was not so. And the wine, shouldn't it be Champagne? But neither he nor Louise liked Champagne particularly. Anyway the wine he had chosen, left to breathe, would go well with the cheese and the bread, and the grapes which Louise had overlooked when she passed through the kitchen. On the bed, nestled amongst the roses was a third envelope. Louise stood there, looking down at the *tableau* before her, trying not to think.

Ben stepped around Louise and was standing in front of a pair of burnt orange curtains fashioned out of shot silk. Stooping down he searched out and flicked on an electrical socket. Louise didn't notice. With the first and second envelopes still in her hand, she bent over to pick up the third, surprised to experience a sudden calmness, almost an unworldliness come over her. An identical thick card lay inside. She pulled it out. The same blue ink, the same handwriting, 'Will you…' She turned slowly to look up at Ben again, but he was pulling apart the curtains and looking out, towards the lake. Thank God, he thought. It was there. It was working. How awful, how embarrassing would it have been otherwise?

Beyond the glass doors were coloured lightbulbs: red, yellow, green, and orange, strung out along a wooden balcony and coming into their own with the encroaching darkness. Hung underneath, individually illuminated by the lights, were large cardboard letters in fairground capitals spelling out the words, 'M A R R Y M E ?'

Ben's immediate thought was to offer a silent prayer to Bill and Peggy, not Louise's answer. Maybe he was confident that he already knew the answer (he was doing the right thing, after all, with the baby and everything). Just as Ben was admiring his sub-contracted handiwork, Louise, from a standing start leapt, into his arms, wrapping her legs around his waist to hug and kiss him. In the process however, her head was thrust backwards with a shocking violence as her forehead struck a brass, punch-holed Moroccan lamp suspended from the bedroom ceiling.

★ ★ ★

A small trickle of blood began to appear from the cut on Louise's forehead, just below the hairline, oozing out as though it had been welling up, building pressure under skin, just waiting for this release. Louise tried to shrug it off, pretend it hadn't happened while all the while thinking, 'Fuck! How FUCKING stupid!' why did she do that? She was so angry with herself. Ben was alarmed and immediately attentive. With her arms still pulling on his neck, he bent forward and licked away the sickly-sweet blood with his tongue. He lowered Louise to the floor and led her to the bathroom.

Louise sat on the toilet seat, still clutching the envelopes and cards, now smeared with small traces of blood. Ben was down on his haunches, dabbing away gently at Louise's forehead with tissue until the blood-born platelets congealed. A cartoon-style bump began to appear. Ben gently kissed the wound and pulled her up. Louise told him not to bother, but Ben disappeared into the kitchen, rummaging through the cupboards for a sticking plaster. Although it throbbed ridiculously, Louise tried to make light of the injury, refusing to let this stupid accident ruin the evening, to overshadow the future memory. She felt a tearful gratitude towards Ben. He must think her so dumb.

"I love you Ben Scott. You are the most amazing person in the world."

"For the millionth time Louise, I've told you not to exaggerate."

* * *

It was some time later before it occurred to them that Louise had not actually answered the question, and that Ben had completely forgotten about the ring.

They sat on the balcony hanging out over the water, late into what had turned out to be a warm evening. The sound of the waves lapping against the boathouse and onto the beach, sheep still occasionally baa-ing, the odd quack from the ducks. The fell opposite silhouetted in high definition. The almost full moon, a misshapen spotlight illuminating a silver path across the lake, all the way to their boathouse. The bottle of red wine was long since empty. Breadcrumbs littered the table, the remains of the cheese just a hardening off-colour smear on their plates, spindly twigs were all that was left of the grapes. Ben fished in his pocket, finally producing the ring.

A blue velvet box. He opened it carefully. Four diamonds, over a thousand pounds each, catching the light from the bedroom. He turned the box around and slid it over the table to Louise, watching her face. Louise's eyes shone, just like the diamonds. She blinked back tears, looked at Ben and wiped her nose with the back of her hand. Ben thought she had never looked more beautiful. Those flashing eyes got him every time. Louise, stared at the ring, nestling there on its satin cushion, said it was the most beautiful thing she had ever seen. Ben, a wide grin consuming his face conceded, as nonchalantly as he could, that it did have a certain, *'Je ne sais croissant.'*

The ring slid on easily, too easily. It was too big. It slipped around, the diamonds getting stuck between Louise's thin fingers. It didn't matter though; it could easily be made smaller. Better this way. Louise kept looking at it, holding her hand at arm's length and waving it around in the light so much that it nearly flew off. She would need to be careful, get it back to London, get it adjusted. Louise reassured Ben that four diamonds were not too many for her delicate finger.

Louise and Ben spoke in whispers late into the night, leaning in to each other over the small weathered table, holding hands, caressing, kissing. A 'Cannonball' Adderley jazz CD playing softly in the background.

They spoke about the new life growing inside her. How weird was that? Articulated rapid, wild, fantastical thoughts about their future together. Where, when and how they would marry. Where they would live. Her job. His ambitions. The dull throbbing ache in her head eased by the narcotic effect of the wine, Louise had never felt such well-being. Ben too. Everything just felt so right, being there together but, how, just how, out of billions and billions of people in the world, had they managed to find one another? How on Earth do these things happen? What mystical fates had conspired to arrange that chance meeting in a teahouse in Camden Town. It became their private joke, 'From a teahouse, via The Roundhouse, to a boathouse.'

★ ★ ★

Ben and Louise finally got up to clear away the detritus of their meal and wipe away red wine stains. They got ready for bed, deciding to leave the doors to the balcony open, the curtains too, so they could hear the water and let in the moonlight. They took up their positions either side of the double bed (left-handed Ben on the right, right-handed Louise on the left) they exchanged intimate looks and smiles, no words necessary. They carelessly discarded decorative pillows onto the floor, turned back the thick white duvet and climbed into the big soft bed. Lying there on their backs, Ben put his arm around Louise's neck and pulled her towards him. He kissed her on the side of the head, carefully avoiding

171

the wound. Louise clung to Ben tightly, conscious of the all new sensation of a ring on her wedding finger.

They lay there awhile in silence, looking up through a skylight directly above their heads, a view of a perfectly clear night sky. They could see the stars and imagined falling into them through the narrow aperture. The sound of an owl reached them from somewhere out in the wood. They didn't attempt to make love; they were tired and happy, content as they were. It had been quite a day and, anyway, they had the rest of their lives.

They stayed like that until Louise was fast asleep, doing that occasional involuntary nervous leg thing she did, and Ben had lost all feeling in his arm and finally had to remove it, trying not to disturb her, blood surging back uncomfortably into the limb before he, too, drifted off.

Some time in the night the sound of torrential rain out on the lake woke them. A storm. Lightning flashes lit up the room followed moments later by thunder amplified by the water. It continued to rain for the rest of the night, but neither Ben nor Louise minded. Not at all. The rain wasn't coming in, and it was romantic lying there with the doors open, breathing in the fresh air, tucked up safe, warm, and dry in the bed. They lay there, listening to the rain, whispering, anticipating the next lightning flash and counting the seconds until the roll of thunder reached them. It wasn't long before their hands started reaching out for each other. God this was exciting!

- XX -

The next day

When they woke again, light was streaming in through the still open boathouse windows. The rain had long since stopped, bright sunshine was dazzling on the water and making patterns on the ceiling of Ben and Louise's bedroom. There was a slight breeze coming in off the lake. The sound of water louder than the previous evening. Lying there in bed they could hear the rigging of the yachts clanging against hollow aluminium masts and booms, sheep baa'ing away in the field next door, wood pigeons cooing from woodland branches and now and again the odd quack. They lay there awhile, reminding each other of the storm in the middle of the night. Giggling. No, they hadn't dreamed it. Making love as thunder, lightning and rain raged out on the lake, a jump-cut illumination of their passion. In each others' arms they replayed all the events of the previous twenty-four hours in their heads. Louise still coming to terms with the idea of a baby and constantly playing with the ring on her finger. But now, today!

* * *

Ben and Louise got out of bed and put on the hooded bathrobes. In unspoken accord they went and stood out on the narrow balcony. The 'Marry me?' sign hung limply, now reading simply 'Mar me?' Two of the letters having disappeared, ripped away at some point during the storm. The string of coloured lights had gone out, fused. It didn't matter thought Ben, they were getting married! Louise had said 'yes' to him. Hadn't she? Of course she would! She's wearing the ring. Just look at her!

* * *

They sat down on the still damp chairs either side of the small table where they had dined so intimately the night before, trying to ignore an obscenely large grey-white splatter of bird shit. They looked alternately out across the lake and then at each other, Louise almost coyly. He could still make her feel that way, especially when she remembered what they had done in bed last night – now that had been a first!

* * *

Ullswater looked magical in the bright morning sunshine. The second longest lake in England (after Windermere) and considered by many, including Ben, the prettiest in the Lake District though, on a fine day, the view atop 'Cat Bells' over Derwent Water ran it close. Ullswater was one of the deepest too, a 200-foot deep trench formed by glaciers in the last ice age. Its snake-like shape formed by different geological strata of granite, slate, sandstone, and limestone. The fells opposite were humbling in their scale: oak, birch and hazel trees at the shore, running up through bracken, gorse and reed beds, more woods, then dark wild grasses and finally, at the summit, scree. A gradation of greens, like a colour paint chart. On the far shore was another boathouse. Not quite a mirror image. 'What scenes are being played out over there?' they wondered. A couple of white-washed farmhouses adjoined to much larger stone barns were the only other signs of habitation and, of course there was the inevitable, irregular grid of dry stone walls enclosing the ancient fields. It all looked so peaceful, so serene.

The lake had been named after a chap called 'Ulf' said Ben, a Nordic chief who once ruled over the area. Louise: 'So it shouldn't it be Ulfswater then?' Ben ignored the question and went on to explain that many Lake District terms came from the Norse settlers of the tenth century, for example a beck was a stream, a dale was a valley, a gill a gorge, and a tarn was a lake. The latter statement unwittingly undermining his weak joke from the day before.

★ ★ ★

Louise gingerly probed at the small red gash and bump on her forehead with a finger. She felt embarrassed but would have felt even worse if she could see what Ben could see from the other side of the table.

"It hurts when I touch it."

"Don't touch it then."

He knew she was tough, but he still wanted to wrap her up in his arms and protect her.

★ ★ ★

Below them, in the water, two blindingly white swans glided up. Their regal demeanour prompting Louise to comment that they knew they belonged to the Queen. They swam so close, directly beneath the balcony, the intricate pattern of their feathers visible. The swans expected to be fed by the inhabitants of the boathouse, they always were. They stood up out of the water, balancing themselves with attention-grabbing wing-flapping, before sinking back down again. A performance put on for the reward of bread. But none was forthcoming. It was all gone, eaten the previous evening. Ben and Louise said sorry to the uncomprehending swans and they eventually sailed away, expressionless black eyes masking the disappointment and confusion they must surely be feeling. At a short distance the swans stopped, their retreating backs to Ben and Louise, and put on a very different performance, a most unregal performance as they plunged their necks into the water to feed on reeds secured to the lakebed, a 'bottoms up' manoeuvre that appeared to Ben and Louise, looking on, to be a retort, a sort of cygnatic mooning.

Next, as though in a preordained order of appearance, an aquatic food chain, two mallards swam up, the luscious green-headed male followed by the dowdy brown female. They quacked ineffectually, they too destined for disappointment.

* * *

There were still no other people to be seen, no one out on the lake yet, no one on board the yachts. It was Louise who suggested it. What better way to start the day?

"Let's go skinny-dipping!"

And with that, she jumped up from the table and re-entered the boathouse, pausing to bend over and smell the roses carelessly arranged in the vase on the dining table. Ben got up and followed.

Barefoot and carrying towels, they trod carefully along the path around the side of the boathouse and across the patio towards the jetty. They took a careful look around, both giggling like little kids. Louise was first to disrobe, revealing her pale slight body with a slight swell in her belly, her dark nipples hardened by the cool breeze. She padded along the jetty and, in one smooth movement, dived gracefully into the lake where she swam a few strokes under the surface before emerging with a gasp, pale buttocks visible just below the water.

She turned to face Ben, still standing on the jetty, watching her. She trod water and pushed hair out of her face.

"What's it like?"

"Oh wow. It's wonderful. So refreshing! It's really okay, once you get in. Come on you chicken."

With that challenge echoing over water (the sound really did carry out on the lake), Ben cast aside his own robe, ran to the end of the jetty and dived in, executing a somewhat less graceful arc than Louise had managed. When he broke the surface, Louise had gone. She was swimming away, further out, an effortless combination of crawl, butterfly and breaststroke, her objective an orange buoy tethering one of the yachts. Ben contented himself nearer to the lakeshore. What was the point in going all the way out there, only to come back again? Louise was right though; it did feel good, especially without swimming trunks. Louise was now heading back towards him. He watched her gliding smoothly through the water. He was so proud of her, he loved her so much. Once again he felt blessed.

Back at the jetty, their feet sinking into the mud and reeds, getting out proved to be not as simple as getting in. There was no ladder, and they had to scramble carefully, trying not to stub their toes, or slip, on the slimy boulders purposely placed to protect the jetty against weather and wash.

With dripping hair, they wrapped themselves in the large bath towels and sat on the jetty wall, Louise's head on Ben's shoulder, and gazed out across the lake at the fell opposite, enjoying the early sun on their faces. Their goose-bumped bodies still tingling deliciously from the lake. On the far shore, the first steamer of the day was heading north towards Pooley Bridge, the wash from the boat reaching the boathouse long after the steamer had disappeared from view, making the yachts at their moorings perform their bobbing dance routine. They were getting a little cold. Time to go in for a hot shower and breakfast.

★ ★ ★

They showered together, soaping and sponging, washing and drying, they put their bathrobes back on to prepare breakfast, moving in and around each other in the kitchen as though they'd been doing this all their lives: Ben halving and juicing oranges, making coffee, Louise poaching eggs, cooking spinach, and preparing a selection of sliced cooked ham: prosciutto, salami, parma, chorizo, iberico.

Breakfast over, and on a second round of coffee, they made plans for the day: they would drive around the lake and go for a walk on Barton Fell, the fell opposite. There was one already earmarked in Ben's book: a moderate walk of around seven miles, it said. It would take them about three and a half to four hours to complete. Perfect. Then they could have lunch in a pub somewhere. Afterwards they would return to the boathouse and go out on the lake in the boat. Outside, the temperature was steadily climbing. It was set to be a lovely day.

★ ★ ★

While Louise was dressing, Ben made a quick call, out on the balcony.

"Bill, it's Ben."

He had never tired of saying that, every time he had called over the past fortnight, unmindful that, for Bill, the flowerpot joke was wearing thin.

"I promised I'd call. Just wanted to thank you and Peggy so much for everything. She said 'Yes'. It's all going swimmingly. Speak soon."

★ ★ ★

Still invigorated by the early morning swim, the hot shower and good coffee, they packed bottled water, two Snickers bars, and two apples into a rucksack, along with Ben's 35mm camera with the telephoto lens, and the guidebook. Ben placed the rucksack in the boot of the Mercedes. They climbed in, snapped shut their seatbelts and exchanged happy smiles. Louise touched Ben's cheek tenderly with the back of her hand. Ben stroked Louise's hair back from her face. He switched on the ignition and lowered the roof once again, still delighting in the low rumble of the V8.

They set off along the driveway, scattering rabbits once again into the hedgerow, up to the main road where Louise got out to open the gate. Emerging slowly and carefully into the blind corner, they headed right, the road closely following the water's edge, the wind in their hair.

★ ★ ★

They drove over a narrow 16th century stone bridge, Pooley Bridge, so narrow the traffic was controlled by lights, Ben spotted a parking place on the other side, just before the former fishing village, once a source of char, trout and perch, but today a centre for tourism. Ben knew that when you find a parking space in the Lake District, you park in it, because there probably won't be another one. He pulled in, next to a two-tone, claret and cream charabanc dating from the 1950s, long sweeping chrome strips along its sides. Beautifully restored and back in service, providing novelty coach trips for passengers of a similar vintage, many of whom now were disembarking and wandering around in the road like unherded cattle.

They got out, retrieved Ben's rucksack and, holding hands, set off into the village, past the shops selling the usual tourist tat; the Lakeland clothing stores; the cafes with unbearably twee names, a few pubs – the Sun Inn looked like a reasonable bet for lunch – and out on the other side, following a riverside path underneath centuries old trees and past shingle beaches. It felt good to get out into the countryside again, especially after enjoying yesterday's walk, but before they could begin to enjoy themselves, they had to pick their way through one of the inherent blights: the garish tents of a sprawling campsite set in a field because the farmer got a better return from campers than he ever could from sheep, let alone a crop on such unforgiving land.

Emerging from the tented village, a refugee camp of holidaymakers, following the guide book's instructions, they turned up a track by a whitewashed farm building and crossed a stile to follow a stone wall until they came to a small stream. They jumped over the water running off the fell and passed through a kissing gate. Finally free. From here they began a gentle ascent up a well-trodden path bounded by gorse, thistle and heather, then over some dry reed beds. The gorse and heather behind and below them, the ground now boulder-strewn grass. At a fork in the path, they followed a sign to Howton, continuing to climb, heading for the copse ahead where they turned sharp left at the edge of the trees and began a steeper climb, along a broad bridle way through wild grasses coloured with pink, yellow and white flowers, like little splashes of paint. There were very few people about – a few over in the distance, no more than dots really, moving about on the fell, only visible because of their bright clothing. Ben and Louise were enjoying the exercise, the simple pleasure, sharing the experience, being together, treading along a path to their own destiny. They enjoyed living in London, but this just gave life a whole extra dimension. Louise was hooked now by what she had taken to calling Ben's 'Lakes larks'.

Still climbing, they skirted the south-eastern border of Barton Wood, passing a lone female mountain biker, standing up in the saddle, pedalling and panting in the opposite direction. They came to a ravine where they stopped to gaze back down the path they had climbed and then out over Ullswater, a thin film of sweat now covered their brows, chests and backs. It really was warm today. Louise pushed the hair out of her face, tucked it behind her ears.

★ ★ ★

She liked the way Ben took control, reading the map, pointing things out to her, leading the way, striding ahead. A clear direction. She trusted him. He was kind and solicitous, yes that was the word she was looking for. And he made her laugh – never underestimate that quality she thought. She knew he was a good man. Her hand went unconsciously to her belly, he would be a good father too she thought, good genes. And she fancied him – just look at him, all male! After the uncertainty, the fear that plagued her when she discovered she was pregnant, that had made her doubt everything, she now felt that whatever happened, it was going to be okay. They were going to wed. They would live happily ever after. 'Til death do us part!

★ ★ ★

They crossed the ravine and climbed the other side, Ben pointing out the Christmas pudding-shape of Dunmallard Hill in the distance. The path then evened out and became a steady walk to what Ben's book described as the 'Cockpit.' This turned out to be a half-hearted circle of tiny stones about 100 feet in diameter. Nothing like the one at Castlerigg, which was what Ben had been expecting. Still, it gave him the opportunity to beguile Louise with his knowledge and theories concerning stone circles.

They walked around the 'Cockpit', it didn't take long, and sat on stones on either side, facing each other. Ben took off the rucksack and placed it at his feet. His back was sticky. Unzipping the bag, he took out his camera and took a series of photographs of Louise, landscape and portrait, sitting there, legs crossed, looking beautiful. He zoomed right in. Then, putting the camera aside, Ben explained to Louise that the purpose of these stone circles was still unknown. No one was even sure when they were erected. It could have been during the Neolithic period he said, or possibly the Bronze Age, maybe around 1500BC. Did they have religious significance, as was most commonly thought? He asked rhetorically. Or did they serve an administrative or commercial purpose? A theory increasingly gaining ground. Ben's guess, he said, was that all were likely. After all, if you've come all this way, gathered (presumably) all these people together it would have been ridiculous to not make the most of such a networking opportunity.

Ben told Louise that the thing that truly fascinated him, the thing he said he just couldn't compute, was that there were stone circles all over Britain. Did these ancient tribes independently come to the conclusion that building a stone circle would be a good thing, bring the community together? Or did someone come up with the bright idea then go around the whole country, on foot, braving encounters with man-eating beasts to disseminate the idea? Or had there been apostles? People dispatched to the four corners of the island? What language did they use? How did they communicate, get the essential idea across? Why was it thought that only stones from Wales would be good enough for Stonehenge? Was this some sort of *exterior* decoration one-up-man-ship, keeping up with the Neolithic Joneses. Louise loved it when Ben went off like this, questioning, expounding, actually thinking about things which others might just stand in front of, take a selfie, upload it, mentally tick it off and move on to the next 'attraction'. Perhaps, concluded Ben, it had been aliens in spacecraft after all, that would make more sense.

★ ★ ★

Louise didn't catch the last of Ben's ruminations on stone circles because, just at that moment, two RAF Tornado jets screamed along the lake in the valley below them, completely shattering the mid-morning air. Ben and Louise were actually looking down on them for the few seconds they were in sight, figure-hugging the topography, dipping a wing here and there, pilots practicing their low-level flying skills. Going impossibly fast. How do they do that? How do they do that? How can they react so quickly to such a rapidly changing landscape of mountains and valleys? Amazing!

Ben got up, contorted himself back into the rucksack that pressed his now clammy-cold t-shirt to him and dissecting the circle, went over to join Louise. Louise put her arm through his and they set off once again, this time heading for a cairn in the distance which marked a crossroads of bridle paths where they would take the one heading virtually straight downhill, back to Pooley Bridge. A glorious panorama was now laid out before them.

★ ★ ★

The Sun Inn was popular. The extensive beer garden having the obvious attraction of a large wooden fort for kids to play in. In fact, kids were everywhere. One, a little girl doing handstands against a wall, her skirt upside down and inside out, was being upbraided loudly from twenty yards away for unladylike behaviour. The girl didn't understand and was too young to care. She continued to practice her technique and upside down staying power. There was a play fight going on between a bunch of kids attacking the fort, and those repelling them with a barrage of pinecones gathered from the trees marking the boundary of the beer garden. Pinecone missiles raining down on the assailants from the fort's tower.

Sitting well out of range, Ben and Louise took in the happy scenes, kids laughing and shouting. Having fun. They decided on what to eat from a laminated all weather menu and Ben headed inside to place their order, leaving Louise to observe mothers interacting with their offspring.

★ ★ ★

Ben had been gone an age. What was taking him so long? He finally reappeared, bearing a tray with their drinks, Stella Artois and a Perrier with ice. A short while later a cheeky young waitress with a broad Lancashire accent came out and served their food. She made a comment to Ben that Louise didn't understand, some sort of in-joke between her and Ben. Louise saw Ben give the waitress that smile of his and he had laughed along with her. They had both completely ignored her. They had deliberately excluded her. Louise didn't like it, her heart started beating faster. Why had he smiled like that? What was so funny? Why was he flirting with that... Louise hesitated. Why wasn't he paying attention to her? She knew she was being irrational. Stop it. Stop it! Control yourself, she said to herself. She determinedly fixed a smile upon her face and looked at Ben, hoping for, what? The smile vanished immediately as all Louise registered was Ben's eyes following the waitress's retreating figure, the white apron not quite meeting at the back, each stride revealing... what exactly? It didn't matter. Oh God, thought Louise. She found her voice. She couldn't help it, her tone was accusing.

"What happened in there?"

"What?"

"What's going on with you and that girl?"

"What? What are you talking about? She's just being friendly." said Ben. "It's how they are up here."

Bewildered and hurt for the second time on this trip. At a loss to understand why Louise was doing this.

Louise thought he looked sheepish, guilty. 'Is this what it's going to be like?' she wondered. It's only going to get worse and worse. She will get fatter and fatter. Her clothes will not fit. She will start waddling, like the ducks at the boathouse. Her body would never be the same again. Ben had told her, had demonstrated so many times how much he loved it. Sometimes in bed, without any warning, he would prop himself up on one elbow and pull back the covers and survey her intently. On these occasions he would take on the appearance of a complete dark stranger to her. His eyes would roam over every inch of her, from clavicle to ankle, up and down, pausing here and there, or returning to trace a light finger over an area of local interest, noting with an almost scientific curiosity whenever he elicited a physical response. A response she would have no control over. She would just lie there motionless under his gaze, unable to move during his inspection. Her body his to violate. Yes, if he wanted to. He could do whatever he wanted. He did. She wouldn't, couldn't, didn't want to stop him. She was powerless, yet at the time knew she had had all the power, it was weird.

All this was going to change thought Louise. He will be repulsed. He'll hide it of course, he won't show it, but he'll be thinking it. He had showed that he enjoyed the concavity of her belly. He would sometimes distractedly run a finger from the top of one hip bone down and round her neat little belly button, picking up speed as he went, climb the other side, turn 180 degrees atop the bony ridge on the other side, before descending once again, a fingertip skateboard. He will never do that again.

"Tell me more about Gnat."

Fucking Hell. Ben had never wanted to know more about Mark. How good/bad he was. The size of his cock. Whether or not she came with him. 'WHY, IS, SHE, DOING THIS!!??' Ben did what men do. He couldn't deal with this. He shut down.

They ate in silence, watching the kids playing before, gradually, things between them returned to normal through a gradual exchange of commonplace observations, pleasantries, inanities. God! Were they turning into their parents after all? Ignoring what had been incomprehensible.

Rested and refuelled, they both just wanted to leave the pub, get back to the boathouse, their love nest, away from other people, take the boat out on the lake. Forget this exchange had ever happened. *Please!*

XXI

A tragedy, compounded

Through a series of affectionate physical gestures, followed by apologies (from both sides), and renewed declarations of love, things did get back to normal. By the time they reached the boathouse, it was as though the 'Sun Inn-cident' (as Ben now thought of it) had *never* happened. It was still warm and sunny but the wind was getting up, it would be chilly out on the lake. They collected their jackets and once more entered the wet dock – no spider webs this time. They released 'Angie' and pushed the boat out.

* * *

"I like the name. Angie. Angel. Angela. We could call her Angela, if she's a girl."

He wants a girl thought Louise, laughing.

"If *she's* a girl?"

★ ★ ★

Out on the lake, Ben kept stopping to take more photographs of Louise. The sun glinting off the surface, the boathouse and lakeshore trees forming the backdrop. Ben carefully lifting the oars out of the rowlocks and folding them inside the boat, trying to keep it steady while he focussed the long lens onto Louise's joyful face, trying to catch an expression in that split second of a camera shutter, the dark flashing eyes, the angle of her head, the graceful neck, the cheekbones. He wanted to capture this moment, these moments. Ben had long ago learned the photographer's secret: take lots and lots of pictures. Great photographs usually coming about through trial and error, serendipity, not by any careful composition or intrinsic technical ability.

They were now out in the middle of the empty lake, the water placid despite the breeze ('Where is everybody?'). Ben was finding rowing hard work.

"This must surely be the worst designed mode of transport ever invented," he complained. "You propel yourself along with your back to the direction of travel. You can't see where you're going! You wouldn't do this on a… bicycle."

Louise said she wanted to have a go. Ben looked at her doubtfully – the boat was heavy to manoeuvre. Seeing his reaction, Louise threw her arms out, saying she knew how to row, and he could then navigate. Ben would not admit it, but his arms and shoulders were feeling a bit weary after the unaccustomed exercise that had brought little-used muscles into play. A short rest would not come amiss, and Louise would realise just how strong he had been up until now.

* * *

Carefully stowing the oars once again, Ben stood up so they could exchange positions. Ben lifted one leg to take a step to the right, over the wooden seat, at the same moment Louise shifted to the same side of the boat. The boat tipped over to the right and then rocked alarmingly as both immediately moved back in the opposite direction, completely negating each other's efforts to stabilise the vessel. Ben lost his balance. At first Louise thought it was comic and was about to shriek with laughter at Ben waving his arms around, trying to regain his balance, his camera swinging heavily around his neck. Then Louise registered the shock on Ben's face as he hit his knee sideways on the top of the hull, his leg unable to bend and, almost straight-legged, almost in slow motion, desperately holding the camera above his head, he toppled into the water.

* * *

Ben was reasonably fit: he had continued to walk and cycle around London even though he now had the car. He played squash regularly, but he had never been that keen on swimming. In fact, once, he had been convinced he was going to drown. He had been in the sixth form, doing his Duke of Edinburgh 'Gold' award. An orienteering trip in Wales, swimming with a group of school friends in a fast-flowing river running through a steep-sided gorge. Ben hadn't wanted to do it. It had frightened him but he had had no option, not in front of his friends.

Ben still remembered the tiredness he felt as fear had drained the strength from his body. He had wanted to stop, catch his breath, but there was nothing to hold on to, nothing to grip. He felt himself being swept away and had started to panic. He had grabbed the shoulders of one of his friends, instinctively pushing his friend down to keep himself afloat but then, miraculously, he managed to find a handhold in the rock, and then a toehold.

Ben had never forgotten that episode and ever since had held a healthy respect for water. Nevertheless, Ben's first thought when he fell into the shockingly cold water, so much colder out in the middle of the lake than it had been that same morning near the boathouse, was to save the precious, irreplaceable images contained in his camera. Pictures that captured a never to be repeated moment in time. Photographs of this beautiful, almost ethereal woman carrying the embryo of his baby protected deeply inside her. His fiancée (though he already thought of her as his wife). The woman he loved unconditionally, with his whole being, and who, amazingly, incredibly, loved him back. The woman with whom he was going to spend the rest of his life.

Ben managed to keep the camera above his head when he went under the first time, but this had left only one arm free to help his legs kick himself back up to the surface where he emerged, spluttering, floundering, his eyes trying to blink away the water. Trying to clear his vision, trying to see her.

When Ben went under, just an upraised arm visible, holding the camera, Louise had the surreal thought that she was looking at a periscope, Ben under water but still keeping an eye on her from his mini submarine.

Ben went down a second time. Panic gripping his whole being. He kicked out, but his movements were heavy and ineffectual, his walking boots filled with water, the fleece lining of his 'guaranteed waterproof' jacket now a sponge. He was still trying to save the camera when Louise finally gathered her wits together. She stood up, nearly losing her own balance. With both hands she tried to lift one of the heavy oars above the gunwale, it was heavy and unwieldy and she first had to pull it out from under the seat then turn it around. By the time she had done so, the boat had drifted a few feet from where Ben had fallen in. Using all her strength, Louise swung round as quickly as she could to extend the oar for Ben to grab. Ben felt the full force of the blow from the flat edge of the oar's blade on his right temple and across his nose.

★ ★ ★

Louise would remain haunted for the rest of her life by the stunned expression on Ben's face. They looked into each other's eyes for the last time. Louise saw Ben wordlessly asking, 'Why did you do that?'

Ben forgot about the camera. Blind panic took over again. He was gasping, hyperventilating, just like all those years ago in the Welsh gorge, only this time there was no friend or rock to cling to. Ben went under for a third time. He tried to hold his breath, but his exertions had used up nearly all the precious oxygen in his bloodstream. Strength-giving oxygen now replaced by carbon dioxide that only led to a stronger and stronger breathing reflex. He swallowed mouthful after mouthful of water.

The surface, he could see it, refracted light above his head, so far up, it was ridiculous, and receding all the time. He was going down and down, all his physical efforts and mental powers not enough. A terrible rushing sound filled his head. He fought and fought with all his being, at the same time he knew that this was how it would end. There was no way he would ever make it back up there, fill his lungs with life-giving air. For a couple of seconds Ben stopped struggling, maybe he thought that if he could just hang on somehow he would float back to the surface. But it hadn't worked, he was going deeper and deeper, just a bit slower.

* * *

More water entered Ben's airways. His larynx constricted and formed a temporary seal, the water going into his stomach instead. When Ben lost consciousness the laryngospasm relaxed and, once more, water was allowed free passage to flood his lungs. Ben drowned quickly and silently.

★ ★ ★

NO, NO... NO!!! This cannot be happening. This could NOT BE HAPPENING! Louise, horrified by what she had done, threw away the oar, the offending weapon. It splashed into the water and floated off. She put her hands to her face and let out an animal scream, the sound carrying far up and down the lake.

★ ★ ★

The kayakers, four of them, were about eight hundred metres away, paddling against the headwind. They froze in mid paddle when the blood-curdling scream reached them. There were people on the campsite over a kilometre away, the campsite Ben and Louise had walked through that very morning, where children suddenly stopped their play, and men erecting tents paused, mallets in mid-air. Women, unpacking, arms full, collecting things, car doors and boots open. All had turned into statues. Couples sitting in folding chairs, wearing hats and sunglasses, turned their faces away from the sun to look at each other in alarm.

* * *

Louise watched in silent horror a constant stream of bubbles, decreasing in size and frequency, slowly burst upon the surface of the water. Ripples by now only just about reaching the hull of the boat that was drifting further and further away from the spot where Ben had fallen in. He'd disappeared. Why didn't he come back up? He'd left her. He promised he would never do that. No. She had sent him away. A deathly quiet descended on the lake. She sat down on the wooden seat. There was an empty space, a void in front of her where Ben should be. He'd become invisible. Where was he? Was he playing one of his stupid tricks on her? She was getting angry with him now. It was no longer funny. Then she felt sure she was dreaming and any moment would wake up in his bed, held in his arms, breathing in the scent from his skin.

* * *

Louise felt a dull ache in her abdomen. It was followed, moments later, by a warm wetness, an uncontrollable leaking between her legs, a dark red liquid soaking the crotch of her new jeans. She fainted, falling forward, collapsing in the shallow pool of water at the bottom of the boat.

* * *

The kayakers came across the oar first, floating detachedly on the water. Then they picked out the tiny rowing boat, empty, drifting aimlessly in the distance. It was only when they got up close they saw that it wasn't empty, inside, lying in the bottom was a tiny figure in a pink jacket. Head tucked in, in a foetal position, red hands pressed between her thighs. Blood, thin red veins suspended in the water where she lay.

The woman did not respond to any of the kayakers' questions. She didn't move. They weren't sure what exactly, but clearly something terrible must have happened to cause that inhuman, blood-curdling, scream. One of the kayakers, a young entrepreneur, out on the lake with his entrepreneurial colleagues, up from London for a few days to celebrate the success of their latest venture, an organic teashop in north London, unzipped his pocket and fished out his iPhone.

* * *

The kayakers were stuck out there now. They should have been at Glenridding long ago. Then, finally, they heard the sound of the rotors slicing the air, shattering the quiet of the lake, reverberating around the fells and across the surface of the water. Then they saw it, appearing out of nowhere, a bright yellow Sea King helicopter, a giant angry wasp, flying incredibly low over the water. It flew straight over them, so low that they all ducked involuntarily. The helicopter dipped in a wide arc and came back towards them, the downdraft causing such huge undulations on the water that the kayakers felt in danger of capsizing and had to steady themselves with their paddles. The helicopter hung in the air above them, the noise incredible, terrifying.

- XXII -

Last chapter

Another text alert. Louise's phone performing a vibrating, crab-like scuttle across the enamel table next to the hospital bed, Louise observed it edge ever closer to the precipice. Vicky again. She would have to reply. She reached over and picked it up. It was almost out of battery and Louise wondered why people said that, 'Out of battery?'. Louise stabbed in her PIN, 2367, the letters on her keypad that spelt out B.E.N.S.

"Where r u? What's going on? R u ok????"

"I hit him with the oar. It was an accident."

Then a second message.

"He's dead. I killed him."

Louise pressed send again and fell back into the pillows, resuming her narcotic stare at the perforated tiles on the ceiling, bloodless knuckles gripping the phone to her hollow, hospital-gowned chest.

★ ★ ★

Louise remained in the hospital in Carlisle for six days. Five nights and six days of care and observation by white-coated doctors supported by blue-uniformed nurses, their cardboard hats secured in place by corrugated hairpins. There had been two interviews with the police, both conducted at bedside by the same kindly policewoman in sensible clothes. Calves and ankles, like upturned skittles, forced into flat shoes. She had been accompanied by an acne-scarred, uniformed junior officer, younger than Louise, who had scribbled away frantically in a notebook. Louise noting that he even licked the end of his pencil.

Louise wondered why the policewoman had asked her over and over about the injury to her forehead. What about Ben's forehead? Even in her confused state, Louise could remember telling her all about it, surely, at the first interview.

Six days before Louise, paler and thinner than he ever remembered, was discharged, still mildly sedated, into the hands of her father.

* * *

Louise had been incapable and, in fact, not even considered when it came to the identification of Ben's body, stretched out cold and naked in a refrigerated filing cabinet in the windowless basement of the Penrith Community Hospital, just a few miles south of where Louise was drifting in and out of consciousness. Ben, the most recent and, by some measure, youngest addition to a grim collection, now just a corpse accessorised solely by a de-humanising blue tag around his ankle. A tag that, surely no irony intended, now obscured a tattooed symbol of the life-giving sun. A tag bearing his now defunct name and the only bureaucratic detail required by the hospital morgue:

Benjamin Edward Scott. 12/11/19XX – 28/08/20XX

For the formal identification a member of Ben's family had been required. Louise was not family. She never would be. Not now. Ben's parents had travelled up by train to Penrith, a four-hour journey spent in numb grief to confirm that a dead body found in a lake was indeed their son. On arrival at the hospital, Ben's parents had been kept waiting as Ben, two floors down, was manhandled by latex-gloved mortuary staff onto a gurney and covered with a white shroud. The parents, already knowing the worst, descended in silence in the special lift and were ushered in through the double doors.

Ben's head and shoulders were exposed, and under the harsh flourescent lights a pale bluish discolouration of the skin was noticeable. Cyanosis. An indication of inadequate oxygenation of the blood.

Ben's parents had clung to each other in their loss, united in a way they had not been for many years. But it would prove to be only temporary. Nearly a year later Ben's father would walk out. Abandon the still unfinished family home. He no longer cared. His heart broken.

★ ★ ★

Louise's father had driven north alone, all the way from Surrey in a resolute, dazed fashion. Bloodless hands on the steering wheel. Over six hours of soulless motorways, M25, M1, M6, hogging the middle lane, only stopping once when the nagging intrusion of the fuel warning light could no longer be safely ignored. His Volvo estate following in Ben's tyre tracks just two days before. Louise's dad had packed a few items into a holdall and reserved a single room in a Travelodge. According to Google maps, it was the hotel nearest to the hospital. Louise's mother had decided against making the journey.

"There's no sense in us both going. Anyway, somebody needs to look after the dog."

Louise's parents had not met Ben. They were aware, vaguely, from e-mails, irregular responses to their own enquiries, some rather cryptic (texting was still a step too far) that she may have met someone special – finally! She had sounded happy in London; the public, i.e. private, school sounded nice. Louise's mother relieved that Louise's desire to move to London had not meant teaching in one of those deprived inner-city 'sink' schools she had read about, where English was the second language and Trojan horses transported girls on FGM holidays, either never to return or, if they did, sporting headscarves and not quite the same ebullient young girls their teachers could recognise from the term before.

★ ★ ★

They had warned Louise, unnecessarily it turned out, that the capital could be a very lonely place. They were therefore happy when Louise announced that she would be sharing a flat with Vicky, her closest friend from school (they didn't really approve of Vicky, but at least she was a 'known known' said her father). They would look out for each other. Her parents wondered when she would next come home to West Byfleet, and whether she would bring this mysterious boy with her. They hadn't seen Louise for a while. They had even thought about coming up to London, to visit, but Louise hadn't invited them, and they really didn't want to intrude.

★ ★ ★

It had come as a complete shock when the doctor told them that Louise would be alright, but he was very sorry to have to tell them that she had lost the baby. Louise's parents had had no idea that Louise had been pregnant. Of course they had no idea about the engagement either. Neither did the doctor, Louise had not mentioned it and there was no ring. Well, it wasn't on her finger, or amongst her effects. Not those retrieved from the boathouse and now stowed in her bedside cupboard, nor those locked away for safe-keeping: a sealed plastic bag, just like the ones at the airport, for your fluids, but larger. A clear bag containing a purse, keys, earrings, necklace, and a labial piercing.

Louise's mother's maternal concern for her

daughter was tempered by what she perceived had been all the secrets Louise had been keeping from her. She had no idea how serious she had been about this Ben, or how serious Ben had been about her daughter. Louise's mother managed to work herself up into a state when she reflected that Louise never told her anything. What kind of mother/daughter relationship was that? Louise practically ignored her when she deigned to come home. Had not told her she was pregnant (PREGNANT! She hadn't even found someone who would marry her, for heaven's sake!). Pregnant with this man's child. This dead man, whomever he was. Or had been.

★ ★ ★

On the slip road into the motorway services, Louise's father drove slowly past a graveyard of abandoned lorries and coaches, cubist silhouettes against the open sky. Glided on past densely parked empty cars belonging to people taking a 'welcome break', having been made aware that 'tiredness can kill'. Where, inside, people queued up to collect plastic trays to carry to plastic tables where they would sit and consume fast food from polystyrene containers and cardboard buckets, washing everything down with ice-diluted Coca Cola.

Not Louise's father. He didn't want to eat. He couldn't. Instead, he searched for a sign, and there it was, a universal pastry-cutter symbol with an arrow. He headed straight into the gents, emerging a couple of minutes later with hands still damp from the

205

ineffective whoosh of a hand-dryer on too short a timer. He then went to fill up with petrol before rejoining the motorway, all these actions performed without exchanging a word, or even eye contact with another human being.

Unlike Ben, Louise's father had not anticipated the motorway delays around Birmingham and opted against taking the toll road (he wasn't a CFO for nothing) but soon realised this to be a mistake when, shortly afterward, he found himself in a frustrating tailback. He hit the steering wheel with his fist and cursed out loud. He just wanted to get to his daughter, she needed him there. RIGHT NOW!

★ ★ ★

The following day Louise's father carefully guided her into the passenger seat of the Volvo before walking around to the other side of the car and getting in behind the wheel. He leant over and secured Louise's seat belt. But before turning on the engine and setting off on the long drive home, he put his hand gently on her cheek and pushed back her hair, just the way Ben had. He spoke gently into her ear, "It's okay Marylou. It's going to be okay."

But Louise, barely willing or able to fight the fog of her drug induced state, knew it never would be. Not again. Not ever.

★ ★ ★

Louise did not attend Ben's funeral where a stupid coffin, containing what? Not Ben, certainly, would disappear on rollers behind curtains into an inferno. Where they would play overwrought organ music. She would not go there to be stared at by complete strangers. To listen to people talking rubbish, seeking their own comfort. She sought nothing less than oblivion. Why should she go? What was the point? She was there when he disappeared below the water, when he died. When she killed him. How could she face Ben's family? Anyway he wouldn't be there she reminded herself. She had seen him into his watery grave. He never came back. She had already buried him, buried him in his favourite place. But why, oh why, didn't she still have his baby, their baby? She had committed the ultimate betrayal of his love. Whatever else, she would never be able to forgive herself for her body's rejection of this physical manifestation of his love for her. The gift that would have kept on giving, the only thing that could have been salvaged. Louise had been robbed of the only possible comfort that, over time, surely would have come. The comfort of knowing that Ben lived on through their child. This was cruel beyond endurance.

* * *

Ben's parents were guiltily relieved that Louise wasn't there. This girl they had never met, intruding on their grief, forcing them to share. This girl who had stolen their son's heart, and then his life. Ben's parents didn't give any thought whatsoever to the miscarried baby.

Epilogue

Having pinpointed the location with GPS, the helicopter radioed the Patterdale Mountain Rescue team and disappeared just as suddenly as it had appeared. A Zodiac launch, shattering the lake's 10km speed limit, its blue light flashing atop a short mast in the stern, reached the kayakers a remarkably short while later. But the rescue divers on board could not find Ben and, after a few hours, with the light fading, decided to resume the search the next day.

Ben was found, finally, around mid-morning at a depth of 120 feet. Police divers having the grim task of bringing his body slowly to the surface and hauling it unceremoniously into the launch where a paramedic was waiting. The paramedic carried out a number of checks before pronouncing Ben dead, causing one of the police divers to snort.

"Course 'e's fuckin' dead."

* * *

The official pathologist's unpunctuated report recorded that Ben died from 'Asphyxia caused by a liquid entering the lungs preventing the absorption of oxygen leading to cerebral hypoxia and cardiac arrest.'

Later, following the inquest, the South and East Cumbria deputy coroner would issue another report. This one contained the verdict 'Accidental death through drowning'. Below the headline could be found a reference to a 'non-lethal blow to the deceased's right temple, consistent with being struck by the blade of an oar.'

* * *

Ben's camera was never recovered. The pictures preserving Ben and Louise's love never seen. It's still there, nearly 200 feet down, at the bottom of a crevice carved out thousands of years ago in the last ice age. Its final resting place. Louise's engagement ring, once so big, now inconsequential, lies not far away.

Afterword

Each year a number of people drown in accidents, often banal, on the Lakes. It's also a popular destination for suicides. Not so long ago, a young man leapt off the side of an Ullswater steamer with a rucksack full of rocks. His body was not found for several weeks.

Afterword

Acknowledgements

I am indebted to Irene Grant, Lisa Connolly, Will Sampson, Paul Cartwright and Mario Aguilar de Irmay for their advice, support and encouragement.

I also wish to acknowledge the following works by John Richardson 'Camden Town and Primrose Hill Past', John Barber 'The Camden Town Murder', Martin Sheppard 'Primrose Hill, A History', Ian Thompson 'The English Lakes, A History', and Hunter Davies 'A Walk Around The Lakes'.

If you enjoyed this book why not browse our recent fiction titles at

www.bookguild.co.uk